ROMANCE

P9-BZN-163

Large Print Lee,M
Lee, Miranda.
The playboy's virgin

WITHDRAWN

STACKS

NEWARK PUBLIC LIBRARY
NEWARK, OHIO

GAYLORD M

THE PLAYBOY'S
VIRGIN

THE PLAYBOY'S VIRGIN

BY

MIRANDA LEE

MILLS & BOON®

All the characters in this book have no existence outside the imagination of the author, and have no relation whatsoever to anyone bearing the same name or names. They are not even distantly inspired by any individual known or unknown to the author, and all the incidents are pure invention.

All Rights Reserved including the right of reproduction in whole or in part in any form. This edition is published by arrangement with Harlequin Enterprises II B.V. The text of this publication or any part thereof may not be reproduced or transmitted in any form or by any means, electronic or mechanical, including photocopying, recording, storage in an information retrieval system, or otherwise, without the written permission of the publisher.

MILLS & BOON and
MILLS & BOON with the Rose Device
are registered trademarks of the publisher.

First published in Great Britain 2000
Large Print edition 2001
Harlequin Mills & Boon Limited,
Eton House, 18-24 Paradise Road,
Richmond, Surrey TW9 1SR

© Miranda Lee 2000

ISBN 0 263 16742 9

Set in Times Roman 16½ on 18 pt.
16-0201-48857

Printed and bound in Great Britain
by Antony Rowe Ltd, Chippenham, Wiltshire

NEWARK PUBLIC LIBRARY
NEWARK, OHIO 43055-5087

CHAPTER ONE

HARRY picked up the four-wheel drive he'd booked at the airport, studied the area maps supplied, bought some food and bottled water from a nearby supermarket, then headed straight out of town.

He had no interest in sightseeing around Broken Hill, despite this being his first visit to the place. He was here for one reason and one reason only. To collect Miss Tanya Wilkinson from the Drybed Creek Hotel and take her back to Sydney with him.

Mining towns—even ones as large and as famous as Broken Hill—held no fascination for Harry.

Neither did the Australian outback. He'd had enough of the damned outback as a kid to last him a lifetime!

Still, it was rather good to return and see it was still the same God-forsaken hellhole of a place. Made him remember why he'd run away

Large Print Lee,M
Lee, Miranda.
The playboy's virgin

6364237

from it all at sixteen. Made him appreciate what he now had.

Within minutes of leaving civilisation there was nothing for as long as the eye could see except flat, frost-burnt plains, bare rocky outcrops and just a smattering of stunted trees.

Admittedly, it was nearing the end of winter. But it wouldn't look much better when spring arrived next week, and certainly not in the summer. In the summer the sun would sizzle down with its fierce bright heat, and any grass the meagre spring rainfall had brought would once again be singed to the outback's familiar brown.

Green was not a colour one ever saw for long in the outback. As for blue... The only blue was the pitiless blue sky.

Harry shook his head at the whole scene. Give him Sydney any day, with its sparkling blue harbour and green gardens, its wonderful bridge and impressive white-sailed Opera House. He'd loved the place on first sight. He'd even loved the noise of the constant traffic. It made him feel alive!

Frankly, he couldn't wait to get back.

His mission here shouldn't take more than one overnight stay before he'd be winging his way home, hopefully with the Femme Fatale heiress sitting beside him.

He only needed her co-operation for a month. Was that too much to ask when the prize at the end of those four weeks was a potential fortune for herself? As it stood at the moment, all she would make out of selling her shares—which was what Richard feared—was a measly couple of hundred thousand dollars. Chickenfeed compared to the pot of gold Harry aimed to dangle in front of her nose.

Harry felt reassured by the description the private investigator had passed on to Richard.

Miss Tanya Wilkinson was in her early twenties. Tall. Attractive. Not a natural blonde.

'A bit of all right' had been the man's overall assessment.

The girl's being physically attractive was in Harry's favour, but it was the early twenties part which was the real bonus. Easier to influence a young woman than some tough old bird with a mind of her own.

Women in their early twenties rarely had a mind of their own, Harry had found. Even if they had, they were still highly susceptible to flattery and persuasion, especially when *he* was doing the flattering and the persuading.

Harry was not vain by nature. But he also didn't indulge in false modesty. He was a good-looking man and the ladies liked him. He also had the gift of the gab, plus a brain which was as devious as it was creative. He could sell anyone anything, if given the chance, which was why his company, Wild Ideas, was one of Sydney's top advertising agencies.

Not the biggest, mind. Just the best.

Persuading some young blonde barmaid from the back of Bourke to do his bidding should not be beyond him.

The fact she was not a natural blonde was a bonus as well. Obviously this girl was no stranger to a hairdresser and cared about her appearance.

There was nothing worse in Harry's mind than one of those bedraggled country women who believed *au naturel* was best!

He shuddered at the memory of his aunt, who'd brought him up—loosely speaking—from the age of eight. She'd never set foot in a hairdresser's. Neither had she ever worn make-up, or perfume, or decent underwear. Or decent anything that he recalled. She'd been grossly overweight and had covered her flab with huge floral tents, all stained with perspiration. Her hair had hung around her face in long, limp greasy strands, its colour an unattractive mix of grey and mousy brown.

No wonder he'd been bowled over by the girls he'd seen when he'd first arrived in Sydney. So pretty, with their beautifully styled hair and perfectly made-up faces.

And they had smelled so good! Whenever they'd come into the Double Bay café where he'd first worked as a waiter, he would stand and sniff the air as they walked by on their clouds of Christian Dior, or Chanel, or whatever scent *du jour* they'd been wearing. When the occasional one had stopped on her way out and invited him back to her place that night, he'd thought he'd died and gone to heaven.

Those initial sexual experiences had given him a taste for the best when it came to women.

He liked them beautiful, and beautifully turned out. Nothing turned him off quicker than a slovenly dressed female.

All his women in the past had been very smart-looking. A lot had been smart, too.

But Harry had eventually found that too much intelligence in his lady-friends was best avoided.

Intelligence was fine in a female employee. Harry had several working for him and they were terrific. Take Michele, for instance. She was smart as a whip. And very attractive. But he'd never have gone near her with a barge-pole.

And he'd been right. She was getting married next month to a chap who hadn't even *thought* of marriage till she'd got her hooks into him. Tyler Garrison had once been the talk of Sydney's social set, a playboy of the first order. A couple of months ago he'd been foot-loose and fancy-free, living the life of Riley.

And now where was he? About to become a husband, promising to love, honour and cherish till death us do part!

The thought that one of his fellow bachelors could betray their brotherhood so swiftly and so completely sent Harry reaching for a cigarette. Lighting up, he dragged in deeply.

Oh, yes, intelligence in a bedmate—although undeniably exciting—came with complications. Such women always wanted more than he was prepared to give. Even if they didn't want you to marry them, they inevitably wanted to *live* with you. Which meant they wanted to keep a very close eye on you, as well as tell you what to do and when to do it, et cetera, et cetera, et cetera.

Harry had decided when he ran away from his aunt and uncle's place that some day no one was going to tell him what to do ever again. No man, and certainly no woman.

He'd reached that status now. He was the boss of every facet of his life and he liked it that way. When friends like Richard asked him if he ever wanted a wife and children Harry would simply smile and say no, that kind of life was not for him.

Hell, no!

If he'd had a wife and family, could he have flown off to Broken Hill at a moment's notice, without having to consult anyone or answer endless questions?

Not in a million years!

Could a husband even consider asking a strange young woman to come back to Sydney to stay at his place for a month?

Good Lord, no!

But *he* could. He could do anything he wanted to do.

And he really wanted to do this.

A surprising realisation, actually. He'd thought he was mounting this mad rescue mission wholly and solely to help Richard. He'd thought he was being a good mate to a man who was facing both financial and marital disaster.

But Harry had discovered somewhere on the flight between Sydney and Broken Hill that helping Richard wasn't his only reason for doing this.

It was the challenge of it all.

And challenges had been seriously lacking in his life lately.

In truth, he'd mastered the advertising game. And he'd made millions in the process. He had everything a materially successful life could offer him. A flash car. A flash wardrobe. A harbourside penthouse. A portfolio of shares and property you couldn't climb over. Plus just about any woman he wanted.

Boring, really.

Rescuing Femme Fatale, however, would not be boring.

It might even be personally profitable, since he owned some Femme Fatale shares himself.

Not nearly as many as Richard, however.

Harry shook his head as he thought of poor Richard and his devastation yesterday.

'The heiress is a barmaid, for pity's sake,' he'd groaned. 'And from woop-woop, no less! There goes my savings, and more. I just can't believe my bad luck in all this.'

Privately, Harry didn't think luck had much to do with Richard's misfortune. Greed, more likely.

Admittedly a couple of months ago Femme Fatale had been a company with a lot going for it, a market leader in the sexy lingerie field with a very dynamic CEO—a woman by the name of Maxine Gilcrest. She'd started the company several years earlier in her own home, running the business as a mail-order service.

In less than a couple of years she'd expanded into retail, listed the company on the stock exchange, then taken her provocative products overseas, to New York and London. Even to stores in Paris! The shares had soared.

Actually, Harry took some credit for the company's rapid expansion himself, since his own agency had handled all their advertising. The various ad campaigns his staff had come up with for Femme Fatale had been great successes!

When Maxine had decided, earlier this year, to venture into perfume, she'd naturally approached Harry to plan an advertising campaign to launch her first exotic scent. They'd hardly got off the ground with this new project, however, when, six weeks ago, in early

July, Maxine—along with her marketing man-ager/lover, also a woman—was killed in a car crash.

When the news of the double tragedy had been splashed all over the papers, shares in Femme Fatale had dipped dangerously. When the details of Maxine's will had been leaked to the press, things had deteriorated further. In it, she'd left her entire estate, including her controlling shares in the company, first to her lover—who had unfortunately pre-deceased her in the accident—and then to her closest female blood relative, whose identity had not been named, or known.

'Whatever possessed Maxine to do such a crazy thing?' Harry had asked Richard when he'd first heard of this extraordinary clause. Richard was the woman's solicitor, as he was Harry's, although they'd known each other for years. Mates from way back.

Richard had shrugged. 'It was an off-the-cuff thing. She'd already left everything to her girlfriend and couldn't imagine such a young woman pre-deceasing her. She argued that if Helen died first she'd remake her will. When

I said what if they died together, she laughed and said what were the odds of that? I insisted that such accidents *did* happen, that if the worst transpired, then relatives—maybe even her ex-husband—could make claims on her estate unless she designated a definite heir. She said no man would ever get a cent of hers, so she said to put down everything was to go to her nearest living female relative. When I asked who that might be she said she didn't know, but surely there was someone somewhere.'

'And is there?' Harry had asked.

'Can't find an obvious one. Her parents are dead, and so is her only sibling, a brother. He was much older, and unmarried. A prospector by profession. Not a very successful one, either. He died of exposure in the Simpson Desert over a decade ago. His and Maxine's parents were English immigrants and came over here alone. Maybe there's someone in England. I've put a private investigator on to the case, but he says it could take some time...'

A month as it turned out. Enough time for more key staff at Femme Fatale to resign, despite the highly recommended management consultant Richard's legal firm had brought in to handle things till an heir could be located.

Yesterday, the shares had reached the rock bottom price of twenty-four cents. Less than a quarter of what they'd been at their peak.

Harry had lost a few thousand dollars but Richard had lost a small fortune!

Finding out yesterday morning that Maxine's brother actually had had an illegitimate child, a twenty-three-year-old daughter who worked as a barmaid in a remote outback pub, had plunged poor Richard into a terminal depression. He was sure the girl would just sell up the shares, especially once she found out that the shares were all her dear aunt's estate contained.

'Would you believe Maxine owned nothing else except her clothes?' Richard had raged to Harry over lunch yesterday. 'Her furnished apartment was rented. Her car was leased. Her bank accounts revealed nothing but an overdraft. She'd poured everything into the company.'

'Happens all the time, mate,' Harry had remarked.

'I don't know how I'm going to tell Liz,' Richard had wailed.

'You haven't told your wife?'

'Not yet. We're not seeing eye to eye at the moment. She already thinks I spend too much money on things that don't matter. She's going to kill me over this. Or, worse, leave me and take the kids with her. I couldn't bear that. You've got to help me, Harry.'

'*Me?*'

'Yes, you. You're the ideas man. Come up with a good one to get me my money back and I'll be your slave for life.'

'Hmm. Can't say that's all that tempting an offer. I like my slaves female. But I'll tell you what, mate. If I can get you your money back, I want that bottle of vintage red you bought at auction last year.'

Harry had look horrified. 'Not the Grange Hermitage!'

'Yeah, that's the one.'

'But…but you'll *drink* it!'

'That's what good red wine's for, isn't it?'

'God preserve me from Philistines! Oh, all right,' Richard had grumbled. 'Anything, if you pull off this miracle.'

So here Harry was, heading for Drybed Creek, feeling more excited than he had since…well, since setting up the Wild Ideas agency all those years ago. The old adrenaline rushes were back, and, quite frankly, he couldn't get there fast enough. Too bad he still had nearly two hundred kilometres to go.

Still, two hundred kilometres wasn't all that far out here. The road was straight as a gun-barrel, and whilst the narrow strip of tar wasn't too good around the edges it was almost devoid of traffic. He should do it in less than two hours.

Harry glanced at his watch. Just after two. He'd be there by four at the latest.

Lighting up another cigarette, he put his foot down. The parched countryside whizzed by in a blur while he wondered what Miss Tanya Wilkinson was doing right at that moment.

Not expecting him to show up, that was for sure. Not expecting his news, either.

Harry had coerced Richard into not calling the girl on the telephone yesterday.

'Let *me* do it personally,' he'd said. Then smiled.

The look on Richard's face had been classic.

'You're not going to seduce the girl, are you, Harry?' he'd asked worriedly.

'Don't be ridiculous,' had been Harry's smooth and suave reply. 'I never mix business with pleasure.'

Not unless it was strictly necessary.

CHAPTER TWO

TANYA caught a reflection of herself in the mirror behind the bar and could have cried. Her hair was ruined. Simply ruined!

Why, oh, why had she tried to do her roots herself? Hadn't the hairdresser warned her once that she had difficult hair to bleach?

But what was a girl to do when she had two inches of near black roots showing and she simply didn't have the time to go into Broken Hill for the day and have it professionally done. When she'd spied the packet of do-it-yourself blonding cream in Mac's Store yesterday, she'd pushed any momentary qualms aside and bought the darned stuff. Then, last night, after the pub had closed and everything was shipshape downstairs, she'd gone upstairs and followed the instructions to a T.

And just look at her! Bright ginger roots, with the rest of her hair the colour and texture of cheap straw. Yet the picture on the box had promised luxurious cream locks which glowed with good health. Of course she hadn't noticed till afterwards that the use-by date had expired three years before.

When she'd come downstairs for breakfast this morning and complained bitterly Arnie had said it looked fine. But what would Arnie know? He was short-sighted, the old dear. Half-deaf too.

Still, he *was* the wrong side of sixty. And he'd had a hard life, trying to scratch a living out of this place, then supporting a kid who wasn't even his kid.

Since the mine had closed down, ten years earlier, Drybed Creek had shrunk from a thriving little community to a one-garage, one-store, one-pub, one-teacher town, with nothing going for it but its petrol and beer. Nothing bred here but the flies. Tanya was the only single girl under fifty in town and had never met anyone in Drybed Creek whom she'd even consider as a candidate for her lifetime partner and the father of her children.

Understandable, considering the type of un-attached male who lived in the place, not to mention the type who frequented the Drybed Creek Hotel. Sweaty, dust-covered jackeroos and singlet-wearing truck-drivers didn't exactly send a girl's heart racing.

Tanya's sights were set a little higher than that!

She'd thought she'd found her dream man a few months ago in Broken Hill. But she'd been mistaken. Bitterly so.

Still, marriage wasn't on her mind right now. Her priority in life at the moment was fixing up several of the pub's run-down bedrooms so that they could take advantage of the increasing number of adventure-bound tourists who often dropped in for a drink and asked if they could stay a night or two. They thought the place was quaint, and rather romantic.

Tanya didn't think there was anything remotely romantic about Drybed Creek. But then, it was home. Familiarity did breed contempt. Maybe the people who lived in Sydney thought the same thing about their city. Yet she thought *it* looked romantic. How many times had she heard complaints about

Sydney's noise, and the traffic, and the drugs, and the crime rate?

Tanya had to admit that they didn't have much noise or traffic in Drybed Creek, except when a road-train rumbled through. As for crime and drugs... The town's sparse population and abject poverty discouraged criminals and drug-pushers.

The only vice in town was the demon grog. And the Friday night dart tournament. A lot of illegal bets changed hands on a Friday night, which might have interested a policeman.

If they'd had one.

The truth was Drybed Creek was practically a ghost town.

Maybe that was what the tourists found romantic in the place, its being the dead opposite to a city. *Dead* being the operative word, in Tanya's opinion. Whatever the attraction, there was certainly some money to be made by offering a bed-and-breakfast deal to deluded travellers.

Arnie, however, was not keen on the idea. He said he didn't want the extra bother. But Tanya had swept aside his objections by saying he didn't have to do a thing. She would paint and prepare the rooms. She would cook the breakfasts and do the extra laundry. When Arnie had pointed out she was already serving behind the bar and doing all their cooking and cleaning, she had argued back that hard work never killed anyone. She was young and strong.

Plus bored out of her mind!

The thought of having the occasional bit of overnight company appealed to her as well. It would be so good to talk to someone who came from somewhere other than Drybed Creek, or any of the stations around!

She hadn't realised till she'd been back in Drybed Creek for a few weeks just how boring it was there, and how few outlets there were for her abundant energy and constantly restless mind. She hadn't minded living there while she was growing up. But when she'd finally left school and taken off to Broken Hill to find a job a whole new world had opened up for her: a world of limitless opportunities.

At first she hadn't really known what she wanted to do. Her HSC pass hadn't been good enough to go to university or college. Although bright, she'd never been able to make up for those early years, when her father had dragged her around with him all over the countryside when she should have been in school.

In the end she'd signed up for an office and computer course at technical college, working as a barmaid at night to support herself. Once her course was over she'd found a clerical job at BHP, but had soon discovered she didn't like being a small cog in such a big wheel. After that, she'd worked at the local council for a while, before landing a job on the reception desk of a busy motel near the airport.

When the manager had left unexpectedly, and she'd been temporarily put in charge, Tanya had finally found her niche.

Being in charge suited her. She was a born boss.

Although never given the title of manager officially, she'd actually been running the motel all by herself when Arnie had come down with a bad flu. When it had developed into pneumonia she'd come back home to Drybed Creek to look after him, and the hotel.

Tanya knew that someday she'd go back to Broken Hill—or further afield still—but she wasn't holding her breath. Arnie pretended he was fine, but she wasn't so sure. He was still coughing in the morning.

On top of that, whenever her back was turned he drank too much, smoked too much, and ate all the wrong food. He needed some-one to keep him on the straight and narrow for a while, watch his diet and make sure he took his vitamins.

Tanya believed if it wasn't for her he'd have died this last winter. Men were hopeless when it came to looking after their own health and well-being. Look what had happened to her fa-ther the moment he'd left her behind with Arnie and gone off on his own!

'Need a nursemaid,' she muttered. 'All of them.'

'Talkin' to yourself, love?'

Tanya glanced up at Arnie, her shrewd gaze narrowing on his cheeks and nose, which were redder than they should have been on a coolish afternoon.

'You've been getting into the Jack Daniels again, haven't you?' she accused, her eyes going to the bottle which looked suspiciously fuller than last night. 'And you topped the bottle up. No doubt with a cheaper brand of whiskey.'

'Hush up,' Arnie hissed. 'You don't want our patrons to hear such things, do you?'

'What patrons?' she returned drily, her hands finding her hips.

Only one person ever graced the bar this early on a Tuesday afternoon, and that was old Jim, the resident town drunk. He was sitting by himself in a dim, dark and distant corner, nursing his usual schooner of Fosters and paying no mind to anyone or anything.

The place was as quiet as a tomb.

Which was why Tanya heard the sound of a vehicle speeding into town. It throttled down when it hit the sixty zone, then slowed even further. Sounded like a four-wheel drive, practically crawling down the main street.

Probably tourists, Tanya decided.

She hoped they were of the variety who found the place romantic. If not, she hoped they were looking for somewhere to stop and have a drink. Or maybe a sandwich. She did a mean club sandwich. Too bad the day wasn't hotter. Tourists and travellers always stopped in the summer, looking for a cool beer or a lemon squash.

Her spirits rose when she heard tyres crunching onto the gravel patch which served as a car park right outside the pub. Shortly, a car door slammed, then some footsteps echoed on the wooden verandah that ran the full length of the front of the Drybed Creek Hotel.

A tall figure finally materialised on the other side of the swinging saloon doors, the slanting rays of the winter sun making a silhouette out of the broad-shouldered and undoubtedly male shape. Whoever he was paused for a moment, before pushing the doors aside and entering the bar, taking a couple of strides before he came out of the glare and into a shaded spot where Tanya could see him properly for the first time.

She couldn't help it. She stared. And then she stared some more.

Because the like of this man had never been seen in Drybed Creek before.

He looked as if he'd stepped out of one of those fashion magazines, from a page advertising Italian suits.

Talk about sleek. And suave. And sophisticated!

He was also strikingly handsome, with a lean, finely sculptured face, a stubborn chin and a highly sensual mouth. His hair was a rich brown, and brushed back from his forehead in an elegantly casual style. It was thick and straight and shone as few men's hair shone out here.

But most attractive of all were his eyes. A light grey and deeply set, they were bisected by a strong, straight nose and framed by a pair of wickedly arched eyebrows which gave him an in-built air of panache and *savoir faire*.

Tanya thought he was drop-dead gorgeous. And so sexy it was sinful.

If it hadn't been for her experience with Robert her little heart would have raced madly at the sight of this good-looking city slicker. If it hadn't been for Robert she might have started worrying about her ruined hair. She might even have made a fool of herself, trying to get such a man to notice her.

Tanya would never have thought she'd be grateful to Robert for anything. But she was at that moment. He'd taught her a severe and salutary lesson about her weakness for men who looked like this, men who would want nothing from a girl like her but the obvious.

Her heart still beat slightly faster as their devastatingly attractive visitor strode in, but nothing even remotely resembling fatuous admiration showed in her eyes, and the only real question in her mind was... *What on earth was a man like him doing here, in Drybed Creek?*

CHAPTER THREE

HARRY momentarily wondered, as he walked in, if he'd made a mistake wearing his new Armani suit. Everyone was staring at him as if he was ET. The geriatric in the corner. The big bald bloke behind the bar. And the girl standing next to him.

Miss Tanya Wilkinson, he presumed.

His eyes went straight to hers, before lifting to her mass of bleached blonde hair. Or what passed as hair. Good grief. If a Sydney salon had done that to a woman they would have been sued! Talk about ghastly.

Still, hair was fixable. He hoped.

Finally, his gaze focused back on her face, her totally unmade-up *au naturel* face.

Not too bad, he supposed, after an initial stab of disappointment. Big eyes. Good cheekbones. Full lips.

Her eyebrows were too bushy, though. And her skin looked dry and sun-damaged.

Still, nothing a day in a top Sydney beauty salon couldn't put to rights.

At least she was tall and slim, with what looked like a presentable bust. Very similar in height and shape to her aunt. With a bit of luck she'd fit into Maxine's extensive and very expensive designer clothes. Richard had said the woman's wardrobe contained several outfits for every occasion. And then some.

The navy sweater and washed-out jeans the barmaid was currently wearing did not project the image he had in mind for the new acting head of Femme Fatale!

He smiled at her as he approached the bar, but she didn't smile back. She just kept staring at him with frowning eyes.

Violet eyes, Harry noted now that he was closer, and the frown was getting darker by the moment.

Harry resisted the temptation to check to see if his fly was undone. He knew it wasn't. But he cooled the smile. Instinct warned him smiles were not going to work on this particular female. Obviously he wasn't her type. Maybe she liked her men rough and ready.

Maybe she didn't like her men traditionally handsome and dressed to kill.

Harry was a bit put out, despite the fact that his plan of attack was to coerce her co-operation with a sensible and businesslike approach, not flattery or seduction. Which was just as well, he decided testily. Because she sure as hell wasn't *his* type, either.

Schooling his face into a no-nonsense, matter-of-fact expression, he dropped his Gucci briefcase at his feet and fronted the bar directly opposite his quarry.

'Miss Wilkinson?' he said crisply. 'Miss Tanya Wilkinson?'

She didn't say a word, just continued to eye him warily.

It was the big bald guy who spoke. 'Who wants to know?' he growled, with equally suspicious eyes. Up close, he looked older than at first sight. But still rather formidable.

'The name's Wilde,' Harry said. 'Harry Wilde. I'm here representing the Femme Fatale company. You may have heard of it. They're based in Sydney and they sell very exclusive lingerie.' Better not say sexy.

The girl finally found her tongue. 'You're a lingerie salesman?' she choked out with a disbelieving laugh.

Harry might have coloured if he'd been capable of it. But being in advertising all these years had rather cured him of reacting to embarrassing moments.

He smiled at her once more, this time drily. 'No, I'm not a lingerie salesman. I'm actually in advertising. I own an advertising agency in Sydney called Wild Ideas. I dare say you haven't heard of it, either.'

'Sorry,' the girl said, not sounding sorry at all. 'I'm also still none the wiser. How is it that you know my name, and what is it that you want from me?'

Harry was taken aback, both by her chilly suspicion and her unexpectedly educated accent. She sounded more like a prim British governess than an outback barmaid.

'That's what I'd like to know as well,' the bald guy joined in.

Harry re-gathered himself and launched into a very businesslike synopsis of Femme Fatale's history and its female boss, finishing with what had happened to the company since Maxine's tragic death. He carefully avoided any revelation about her aunt being a lesbian. When he got to the part where it turned out Maxine had left her estate to her nearest female relative, who just happened to be Tanya, the girl looked simply stunned.

It was a pleasant change from frosty suspicion.

When he produced his letter of introduction from Richard's legal firm, along with a copy of her aunt's will, she read both very carefully, shaking her head all the while. When she'd finished, she passed the papers on to the bald guy, then looked up at Harry with shock still in her face.

'I knew Dad had a sister somewhere,' she admitted. 'But he never wanted me to have anything to do with her. He said she was wicked.'

Harry's eyebrows lifted at this. Was it Maxine's being a lesbian that her brother had disapproved of, or her making a living by selling sexy lingerie?

'Are you saying Tanya here's an heiress?' the bald guy asked. 'That she's *rich*?'

'She is and she isn't,' Harry returned. 'Unfortunately, Maxine left no personal assets of property or goods other than a very nice wardrobeful of clothes. She was, in fact, in a small amount of debt when she died. Miss Wilkinson will, however, inherit a large amount of shares in her aunt's company.'

'Wow! That's great!' the bald guy enthused. 'Did you hear that, love? You're rich.'

'I don't think so,' the girl commented thoughtfully, 'From what Mr Wilde's just said, those shares aren't worth much at the moment.'

Harry wasn't about to lie to her. Not yet, anyway. 'I suppose that depends on your point of view. They're not worth a fraction of their real value. But you'd still have close on two hundred thousand dollars if you sold your shares on today's market.'

'Two hundred thousand!' she gasped, and Harry realised instantly he was in big trouble. He should have known the moment he drove into Drybed Creek that two hundred thousand would sound like a lot of money to anyone who lived in this dead-end dump.

The girl grabbed the man next to her by his big arms and practically jumped up and down, her eyes alight with joy. 'Did you hear that, Arnie? With two hundred thousand I could fix up this place and make it into something really classy. I could have *en suites* put in to some of the bigger rooms. And air-conditioning. And—'

'Now wait a sec, love,' the man named Arnie interrupted, putting a swift stop to her excitable plans. 'I couldn't let you do that. This money's yours, not mine. You won't be living here at the Drybed Creek Hotel for the rest of your life. Not a girl like you. You should put it in the bank for a rainy day. Remember how you've always said you wouldn't be like your father? Never saving a cent or owning a home of your own.'

'Yes, that's true…'

'But first you should spend a little on something you really want. A holiday, perhaps. How about a trip to Sydney? You've *always* wanted to go to Sydney.'

Harry was beginning to like this Arnie. He was just about to open his mouth and launch into his proposition when the girl got in first.

'How can I go to Sydney when you need me here? No, no, Arnie you can't get rid of me as easily as that. No, I'm staying right here till you're *really* well. And I don't want to hear any more rubbish about it being my money and mine alone. What's mine is yours. No, I'm going to sell those shares straight away, then use the money to turn this place into a proper B and B.'

Harry caught a glimpse of dismay in Arnie's eyes, and twigged to the fact that the poor guy was sick to death of his barmaid running his life, and his pub. Though obviously she was more to him than just a barmaid. But what? Arnie was old enough to be her grandfather! Harry cringed at the thought they might be lovers. But stranger things happened, especially when you lived out here in the boondocks.

Whatever their relationship, Harry was glad he'd found himself an ally. Because he could see she was a stubborn little Madam. Smart, too. Nothing at all as he'd imagined.

And there he'd been, so confident she'd be a push-over in the persuasion stakes!

Still, her secret hankering to see Sydney was a plus. And he hadn't as yet tapped into that failsafe human weakness. Greed.

'Unfortunately, it's not as simple as that,' he intervened. 'Firstly, Miss Wilkinson can't sell the shares till the will is properly processed, which will take a few more weeks. Secondly, you might find that by then it will prove very difficult to find a buyer for such a big block of shares in a company which is in a pretty precarious state at the moment.'

'Oh,' she said dispiritedly.

'I have a plan, however,' Harry continued, 'which hopefully will salvage your aunt's company and put a bit of life back into those shares. Perhaps even make it attractive enough for a takeover bid. But I really do need you to accompany me back to Sydney, Miss Wilkinson.'

'But how can I? Arnie's been sick and—'

'And I'm right as rain now,' Arnie broke in firmly. 'Honest, love. *Listen* to what the man's sayin'! Chances like this don't come along every day of the week, you know.'

'It would only be for a month,' Harry pointed out reasonably. 'One month out of your life during which you'll get a free trip to the greatest city in the world, and possibly the biggest financial windfall of your life!'

'But how will my coming back with you for a month achieve that?' she asked, with a mixture of puzzlement and wariness in her voice. 'I mean…what could *I* do?'

'It's like this, Miss Wilkinson. As your aunt's heir apparent, till you actually sell those shares, you're in charge of Femme Fatale.'

'*Really?*'

Harry could see that the idea both startled and intrigued her.

'Yes, *really*,' he repeated firmly. 'You've inherited a controlling number of shares, which gives you the say-so on how things are run at your aunt's company. Frankly, at the moment Femme Fatale desperately needs you, Miss Wilkinson. Your aunt's executors brought in a management consultant to handle things until an heir was located, but he's a man. I have a strong suspicion that your aunt's largely female staff resent his being in charge. They're used to a woman boss. I'm hoping that with you at the helm it could be a different story.'

The girl frowned, then gnawed at her bottom lip. 'But I know nothing about the lingerie industry…'

'That's where I come in. My advertising agency has handled the Femme Fatale account for a few years and I've gleaned quite a bit about your aunt's business in that time. I'll be your secret guiding hand. Your right-hand man behind the scenes, so to speak.'

She still looked unsure, which was understandable. As naturally intelligent as she was, underneath she was just a simple country girl without the background or business nous for such a job. Running a bush pub was a far cry from running Femme Fatale!

But beggars couldn't be choosers in this instance. It was her or no one. And she didn't really have to run the place. Just be *seen* to be running it.

'What harm could you do?' Harry pointed out persuasively. 'The company's going under as things stand. Look, the annual general meeting is in a month's time. If you can instil some confidence in the place leading up to that meeting, then present a strong leadership figure there on that day, the shares are sure to rally. They might even get back to somewhere near the price they were before your aunt's tragic demise. Either way, their value is sure to rise. At which point you could sell all your shares, then come home here with a real fortune in your bank account. As I said before, it's only a month out of your life.'

Harry could not believe it when she still hesitated. What was the matter with the girl? Didn't she have any guts or gambling spirit? Surely she wasn't still worried about leaving dear old Arnie! He wanted her gone. That was perfectly clear.

'Say everything goes as you plan, Mr Wilde,' she said seriously, 'and the shares rally. What will happen to the company after I sell up and leave?'

Harry was flabbergasted by her concern. My God, what did it matter?

'It'll sink again, won't it?' she went on worriedly. 'And all those poor people at Femme Fatale will probably lose their jobs.'

Harry could not believe his bad luck. Of all the barmaids in all the world, he had to tangle with one who had a social conscience!

'Not necessarily,' he said, smiling through clenched teeth. 'During the month you spend in Sydney you could make sure good executive staff are hired to give the company a fighting chance of survival.'

'What's wrong with the executive staff they already have?'

'They're resigning at a rate of knots.'

'Oh, I see. Yes, I see.'

Her eyes narrowed on him and Harry suddenly felt as if he was some nasty creepy-crawlie under a microscope. 'So tell me, Mr Wilde, what's in this for *you*? I mean…you've certainly gone to a lot of trouble, coming way out here yourself. Drybed Creek is hardly a hop, step and jump from Sydney. Is the Femme Fatale advertising account worth that much to you?'

Harry only just managed to hide his escalating frustration! Lord protect him from females who had more brains than they had a right to have and were cynical to boot! Why couldn't she have been a dumb blonde bimbo with nothing but dollar signs in front of her eyes?

Still, Harry was nothing if not flexible when it came to business. He also always used every card in the pack when playing the game of getting what he wanted. 'May I speak to you in private, Miss Wilkinson?' he said in a low and confidential voice.

'I think perhaps you should call me Tanya,' she replied, with an unflattering degree of reluctance. 'But anything you have to say to me you can say in front of Arnie. He's been my surrogate father since my dad died. There's no secrets between us.' And she linked arms with the big bald man beside her.

Harry winced at the look of warmth and sweet affection which passed between them. He was glad they weren't sexually involved, but he always felt uncomfortable in the presence of overt gestures of love. When Richard and his wife were getting along they were so mushy together it was truly sick-making!

'I sure have,' Arnie returned firmly. 'And I'm not goin' anywhere. So speak up, Mr Wilde.'

Harry smiled through gritted teeth. 'Do call me Harry.'

'Great. We don't stand on ceremony out here. So, what's the real gin, Harry?'

Harry dragged in a delaying breath and let it out slowly. 'You're right. I *have* gone to a lot of trouble—and expense—to come here personally. But not for myself. The rise or demise of Femme Fatale will make no real difference to me, or my advertising company. Wild Ideas is already hugely successful, and I have no need of one more account, especially one as dicey as this.'

He fixed his gaze on the girl's face for the moment, looking deep into her big violet eyes. Her returning expression was still wary, and Harry decided to play his trump card.

The truth.

'I won't pretend to you, Tanya. I don't really give a damn about you, or your inheritance. Hell, I don't know you from a bar of soap! I've come here to save someone I *do* care about. From financial ruin. His name is Richard Mason and he's one of the partners in the legal firm which represents your aunt and her company. He also happens to be my best friend.'

Harry hesitated, strictly for dramatic effect.

'Go on,' the girl prompted eagerly, and Harry knew he had her.

His sigh sounded worried, but hid a degree of relief. 'Richard has a huge holding of shares in Femme Fatale. Unfortunately purchased when the shares were close to their highest price. He was a fool to buy so many, and especially foolish to borrow to buy even more. But he thought it was a safe investment for his family's future. Richard, unlike my bachelor self, is a devoted family man, with two of the sweetest kids. A boy and a girl. Brett and Tess. I'm actually Tess's godfather.'

True, though rather perverse, since Tess's christening had been Harry's only visit to a church since his own christening as a baby.

Harry shook his head sadly and dropped his gaze to the bar, lest his listeners spot any lack of sincerity.

'If Femme Fatale goes under,' he said bleakly, milking the situation for all it was worth, 'then so does Richard. Possibly along with his marriage. It's going through a bad patch and this might be the last straw where his wife is concerned. He's afraid she might leave him when she finds out what he's done, and take the children with her. I can't sit back and let that happen. I *won't* let that happen,' he added, thumping the bar with a closed fist. 'Not while there's breath in my body.'

Harry worried he might have overdone things, till he looked back up and found the girl regarding him with much softer and almost apologetic eyes. He felt like preening under her new admiration, only just managing to continue to look fiercely determined and not smugly triumphant.

'You hafta admire a man who stands by his mates,' Arnie pronounced. 'You've gotta go to Sydney now, love,' he directed at his surrogate daughter. 'I know you. You couldn't live with yourself if you didn't try to help Harry's friend. Not when the happiness of a family is at stake. And there's no shame in tryin' to make some extra money for yourself while you're at it, is there, Harry?'

A man after his own heart. 'Certainly not!' Harry reassured him firmly.

'You're right...' the girl said, if a little disconsolately. 'I know you're right. It's just that...'

'You'll worry about me,' Arnie finished gently.

'Yes.'

'That's silly and you know it. I'll be fine. Dolly Walton said she'd help out if I ever needed help.'

The girl's eyes widened, her mouth opening before pressing shut with obvious disapproval.

'You stay right away from Dolly Walton,' the girl ordered. 'For heaven's sake, Arnie, she's already married every half decent bloke within fifty miles of Drybed Creek. And she's outlived all of them. Talk about the black widow!'

'Dolly's a nice woman, Tanya, my girl,' Arnie said sternly. 'She's just been unlucky, that's all.'

Harry reckoned from the sounds of things that any man who tangled with this Dolly was the unlucky one. But who was he to say anything and possibly spoil the splendid progress he was now making?

Still, he would have to remember in future that the key to this girl's co-operation was not flattery or greed, but sympathy. She had a soft heart underneath that surface cynicism.

Harry wondered what man had hurt her in the past to make her regard him with such wariness to begin with.

'Well…all right,' she said at last. 'But I can only be away a month!' she added, with a frowning glance cast Harry's way. 'Not a single day longer!'

'I don't know how to thank you enough,' Harry gushed, leaning over to grasp her hand in his and trying not to smile too broadly.

CHAPTER FOUR

TANYA stared first at his smiling mouth, then down at the strong hand gripping hers, with its long strong fingers and blunt but neatly manicured nails.

There's no need to panic, she told herself. So your heart just did a huge flip-flop, and your stomach is at this moment twisting into a sickening knot.

So what? It doesn't mean anything except that you find the man attractive. Haven't you learned yet that a fluttering heart and churning stomach aren't symptoms of anything but your female hormones firing up once more? It doesn't mean you're falling in love again.

You're just acting like a normal red-blooded Aussie girl. Get used to it!

But it was hard to get used to feeling like this after twenty-three years of feeling nothing remotely resembling physical passion for any of the country boys she'd dated. And especially hard when the one other man who'd managed to kick-start her sexuality from an apparently frozen zero to a highly flammable state had also been a handsome businessman from Sydney.

Tanya found it dismaying that she could be blindly vulnerable to a certain type of male. She didn't like the thought that she could be turned on by any suave, suit-encased city slicker who crossed her path. Especially ones who didn't fancy her in return.

Tanya knew when a man fancied her. She could read the signs. There was that tell-tale gleam in their eyes when they looked at you; that flirtatious tone in their voice; the compulsion to flatter and compliment you to death.

Robert had fancied her like crazy.

Harry Wilde did not fancy her at all.

So don't go making a fool of yourself over him like you did Robert!

Gathering herself, Tanya swiftly extracted her hand from his then lifted cool eyes. 'I wouldn't be too grateful just yet,' she said ruefully. 'The people at Femme Fatale might take one look at me and think I'm such a ning-nong they'll all resign on the spot.'

Arnie laughed. 'You? A ning-nong? Why, love, you're the best little businesswoman I know! You'll have that place shipshape before Harry can say Jack Robinson!'

Tanya didn't share Arnie's confidence. The news about being her aunt's heir was still making her head whirl. And the prospect of going to Sydney with Harry Wilde and trying to run this Femme Fatale firm—even for one month—was so daunting she felt nauseous thinking about it!

Aside from her knowing nothing about the way a lingerie company would work, there was the problem of her appearance. How could she possibly go to Sydney with her hair the way it was? She'd just die of embarrassment!

But she'd given her word. And Harry had been so delighted.

Tanya realised with an annoying niggle of exasperation that she might do anything to make Harry Wilde that delighted with her again.

And to have him take her hand in his again.

And to have him smile at her like that again.

Lord, but she *was* a complete fool where men like this was concerned! And all these years she'd thought herself so sensible where the opposite sex was concerned. Nothing like some of the silly girls she'd met in Broken Hill. Or her own poor pathetic mother.

But give her a suave city slicker in a suit and all her much-vaunted common sense flew out of the window.

How humiliating!

'What about my hair?' she said abruptly.

'Not your hair again,' Arnie groaned. 'There's nothing all that *wrong* with your hair, love.'

'I have no intention of going anywhere with hair like this,' she muttered stubbornly. 'I usually go in to Broken Hill to have my hair done,' she told a curious-faced Harry. 'But last night I stupidly used this do-it-yourself stuff and it didn't work the way the packet said it would, as I'm sure you can see for yourself.'

'I did notice the roots were a different colour to the rest,' he returned, with great diplomacy and understatement, she thought. 'But

Arnie's right. Nothing a good hairdresser in Sydney can't fix. I'll line up an appointment for you the moment we get back tomorrow.'

'*Tomorrow!*' she exclaimed, half-horrified, half-hopelessly excited. 'You want me to go to Sydney *tomorrow*?'

'There's no time to be wasted, I'm afraid.'

'No. No, I guess not,' she agreed, forcing herself to sound calmer. But inside she was still very agitated over the storm of conflicting feelings besieging her.

Fear of making a fool of herself in more ways than one eventually gave way to the fizz of excitement. A whole month in Sydney with Harry Wilde by her side! How could she possibly not want to go?

'You don't have to worry about a thing,' Harry said reassuringly, no doubt having spotted some panic in her eyes. 'I've already booked two tickets on tomorrow afternoon's flight from Broken Hill. If we leave after breakfast in the morning we should get there in plenty of time. Now, I presume you have a room I can stay in for tonight? This is a hotel, after all.'

Tanya exchanged an eyebrow-raised glance with Arnie.

'I'll pay for it, of course,' Harry added, frowning at both of them.

'It's not a matter of money, mate,' Arnie informed him. 'It's a matter of a bed. Tanya here's been doing up all the rooms. All the furniture's piled up in the centre of the rooms.'

'There's one which *might* do,' Tanya conceded. 'If you don't mind the smell of paint and no curtains. I just finished it yesterday.' She'd shifted the furniture back herself, not wanting to ask Arnie, who had been down in the cellar at the time. It had been a struggle, but she'd managed.

'A bed's a bed,' Harry said with a shrug of his elegantly suited shoulders. 'And it's only for one night. I'll keep the windows open.'

'Sensible man,' Arnie said.

'I'll go make the bed up,' Tanya said.

'And I'll go get my things.'

'No rush,' Arnie jumped in. 'Care for a beer on the house first?'

'Don't mind if I do.'

'If you'll excuse me for a few minutes,' Tanya said, and dashed off, relieved to have a few minutes away from Harry's dazzling presence and far too sexy smile.

Still smiling his satisfaction, Harry slid up onto the nearest bar stool and watched Arnie expertly pull a beer, then pour himself half a glass of straight Scotch.

'Now that it's just you and me,' Arnie said as he slid the beer glass into Harry's hand, then swept his own drink up to his mouth for a quick swallow, 'I'd like to talk you about this here trip to Sydney. Now, I've got this good mate who owns this pub down near Central,' he went on between gulps of Scotch. 'I'll give him a buzz and see if he'll let Tanya stay there. She's never been to a big city before, you see, and he'd keep an eye on her for me.'

'Er…I don't think that's such a good idea, Arnie.'

'Why not?'

'How long is it since you've been to Sydney?'

Arnie scratched his bald head. 'About fifteen years. Give or take a few.'

'Believe me when I say it's changed since your last visit,' Harry informed him drily. 'A pub down near Central is not the place for a girl like Tanya to stay for a single night, let alone a whole month, no matter how many eyes are kept on her.'

'A bit unsavoury round there nowadays, is it?'

'You could say that.'

'Mmm. Well I'll take your word for it, Harry. I guess you'd know. You live there. And Tanya's a good-lookin' girl. No doubt about that. The fellas are always sniffin' around her, I can tell you. But she's a good girl. A *very* good girl, if you get my drift.'

Harry nodded that he did, though privately he wondered if Arnie might not be suffering from a degree of paternal delusion.

Okay, so Tanya wasn't quite Miss World material.

But underneath the straw frizz and ginger roots she was pretty enough, and twenty-three years old to boot. She also had a job which constantly put her into the company of half-drunk males with more on their minds than guzzling beer.

Harry didn't think there were too many attractive twenty-three-year-old virgin barmaids around.

'Actually, I was going to invite Tanya to stay at my place,' Harry said smoothly. 'I'm the one who's asked her to come to Sydney, after all. It wouldn't be right for this trip to cost her anything. I have a very nice apartment near the city with plenty of room. She'd have her own bedroom and *en suite* bathroom. If you're worried about her safety, I promise you that she'll be chaperoned by me personally everywhere she goes. I won't let her out of my sight.'

Arnie's mouth twisted in a wry grin. 'That's great, Harry, but who's going to save her from you?'

Harry's beer glass hit the bar with a thud. 'What?'

'You heard me.'

'I guess I did. But I'm not sure I like what I heard.'

'How old are you?' Arnie quizzed.

'Thirty-five. Why?'

'You're not married, right?'

'No. Not my scene.'

'Gay?'

Harry smiled. 'Not that I know of.'

'Got a lady-friend at the moment?'

Harry always had a lady-friend. 'Sure do.'

'That's good, then. But I still want your word that my little girl comes back to Drybed Creek the same way she leaves it.'

Harry was a bit put out by this demand. Did he look like an unconscionable rake?

Okay, so he wouldn't be *his* first choice as chaperon for *his* daughter, if he had one. But, truly, Arnie had nothing to worry about. Harry found Arnie's little girl very resistible.

Even if he and Renee shortly parted company—and he suspected their affair had just about run its course—he had scads of beautiful sexy women in his little black book who would be willing to step into Renee's place at a moment's notice. He had no need to seduce little Miss Prickly from the bush.

'You have my word,' he said firmly.

'Shake on it.'

'Fine.' And he did.

'Your word on what?'

The object of their discussion seemed to materialise out of thin air, startling them both with her wary-sounding question.

Harry had to smile at Arnie trying to hide his Scotch behind his back. 'I've promised Arnie to take care of you in Sydney,' he said, doing his best to distract Arnie's eagle-eyed minder. 'You'll be staying at my place, of course.'

'Are you sure that'll be all right?' she asked, frowning. 'I mean…do you have the room?'

Harry's penthouse could probably have accommodated a football team, but he decided to downplay its size and grandeur for the moment. More to alleviate any worry on Arnie's part rather than a reluctance to impress Arnie's 'little girl'.

Nothing about him impressed her, anyway, except his willingness to help Richard. And that tiny burst of admiration hadn't lasted for long. Within seconds of his basking in her sudden warmth she'd been snatching her hand away from him as if he was some low-grade slime.

Not that it mattered. He could endure a dent to his male ego occasionally.

Still, it might be interesting at some time to find out exactly what kind of male she liked. If she liked any, that was. Maybe Arnie was sure of her virtue because she was a rabid man-hater, like her aunt.

'Harry said he had a guestroom,' Arnie chipped in.

'A house, is it?' she asked him coolly.

'No, an apartment,' Harry replied. 'At Kirribilli. That's just over the Harbour Bridge, near North Sydney.'

'Sounds handy.'

'It is. From the balcony you can see the bridge on your right, and you look straight across the harbour to the Opera House and Circular Quay.'

'Tanya's always wanted to go to the Opera House, haven't you, love?' Arnie said.

When she flashed Arnie a sharp glance Harry realised she might want to go to the

Opera House, but not necessarily with yours truly.

'I'll see if I can organise something,' he offered politely, before tipping the rest of his beer down his throat and sliding off the stool. 'I'll go bring my things in, if the room's ready.'

'It's as ready as it'll ever be today,' she returned drily.

Harry bent to pick up his briefcase then strode off outside again, oblivious of Tanya staring after him and Arnie watching her with a thoughtful expression on his whisky-flushed face.

'He's a good lookin' bloke, our Harry, isn't he?' he said in a laconic tone.

Tanya knew Arnie too well to be fooled. He'd looked after her and her virtue like an old mother hen since her father had died. Done a good job, too. Though it hadn't been very hard during the years her female hormones had lain dormant and she'd found nothing overwhelmingly pleasurable in the attentions of the opposite sex.

Till Robert came along...

She sighed. 'Say what you have to say, Arnie. And be quick about it. He won't be long.'

'Fair enough. Watch yuhself with him down in Sydney, love. Harry's a good bloke, but he's still just a man. Not the man for you, though.'

'Oh, really?' Her hands found her hips, as they always did when she was ruffled by a situation or an opinion. 'And why is that, pray tell? He's single and I'm single and it's a free country.'

'Yeah, but he's the kind of single who aims to stay that way. And you're not.'

Tanya's heart gave a little lurch. 'How do you know he aims to stay single?'

'He said so.'

Tanya frowned, wondering why a man of Harry's seeming depth and sentiment would make such a decision. It was clear he really liked his friend's two kids, especially the little girl. Why wouldn't he want kids of his own? And a wife who loved him? And a real home to come home to every night, one with a big yard and a dog, not some high-rise apartment with a miserable little balcony?

'He's a confirmed bachelor, my girl,' Arnie stated firmly. 'And a bit of a lad with the ladies, if I'm not mistaken. So I repeat…watch it with 'im.'

Tanya sighed. 'You're making too much of all this, Arnie. Okay, so I find Harry attractive. What girl wouldn't? But I'm not about to make a fool of myself. I promise you.'

'Good, because he's already got a girl-friend.'

Despite everything she'd told herself—and Arnie—her heart still tightened at this news.

But she handled and hid her disappointment well. If Robert had left her one lasting legacy it was not to wear her heart on her sleeve as she had with him.

'No kidding,' she said, smiling wryly. 'I won't have to worry about him chasing me round and round his apartment, then, will I?'

'A man like Harry doesn't have to chase women. The silly fools throw 'emselves at 'im.'

'Arnie, have you ever known me to throw myself at a man?' Fortunately Arnie didn't know anything about her affair with Robert.

She'd been too ashamed of herself to tell him. She'd tried not to be easy, but it had only taken Robert a few wretched dinner dates and some minor groping before she had gone willingly with him to his room, panting for more.

If it hadn't been for the fire alarm going off in the motel that night…

Tanya shuddered to think of how close she'd come to going all the way with that creep. Talk about being saved by the bell!

'Yeah. You're a pretty sensible girl,' Arnie conceded.

'Then stop going on about it,' she said sharply. 'Now hush up. He's coming back.'

CHAPTER FIVE

HARRY didn't think the room she showed him smelled too badly of paint. Perhaps because it was large and both the windows and French doors were open.

The bed was big and solid, the wooden floor polished and the walls a deep blue, trimmed with white. Two oak bedside chests flanked the bed, along with twin multi-coloured rugs. A large matching wardrobe with three doors stood against the wall opposite the bed. There were no pictures on the wall, but Harry didn't care about that.

The bed was what mattered most. It looked country and comfy, with four snow-white pillows and a navy and floral quilt. He'd been up since before the dawn, and suddenly felt bone-weary. A lie-down would be good. Yet his watch showed only four-thirty-five.

Harry couldn't remember the last time he'd felt like a nap in the afternoon, let alone taken one. Maybe it was the full-strength beer hitting his near empty stomach. Or adrenaline withdrawal after the success of his mission.

'You've done a good job on the room,' he complimented as he swung his overnight bag onto the straight-backed chair in the corner nearest the door.

'Thank you,' she replied, with still-stiff politeness. 'There's a bathroom at each end of the hallway. If you use the one to your right, you won't have to share. I'll go get you some clean towels.'

'Thanks.'

When she'd hurried off, Harry stared after her for a few moments. Why didn't she like him? Was it something he'd said or done, or just the way he looked? In truth, she'd seemed against him from the moment he'd walked through those saloon doors.

Harry vowed to find out why. But not today. He didn't want to risk putting a spanner in the works before getting her safely on the road tomorrow.

With a somewhat weary sigh, he took off his silk-lined grey jacket and hooked it over the back of the chair, then strolled out through the French doors and onto the wide wooden verandah.

Most bush pubs were designed the same way: solid two-storeyed buildings with stone or brick walls, corrugated iron roofs and wide wooden verandahs running the full length of the building's façade, both upstairs and down. Downstairs, the verandahs were always open, with long slab seats resting against the outside walls. Upstairs, they had iron-lacework railings which were mostly painted green, like this one.

Harry wrenched his tie loose and undid the top button of his white shirt whilst he stared out over the top of the town's derelict shops and houses towards the far horizon. There, the winter sun was rapidly sinking in the sky and turning a deeper gold, its rays brushing the landscape with rich colours ranging from orange to deep red and burnt siena.

He had to admit that if the outback had anything going for it, beauty-wise, it was the sunsets. Plus the clear night skies which followed. Black as the ace of spades, they were, and dotted with stars the like of which you never saw in the city.

But spectacular sunsets and glorious night skies didn't do a thing for you if you were lonely and wretched...

Harry leant his forearms against the railing and let the sunset's beauty wash over him, all the while thinking he couldn't wait to get back to Sydney.

'I've put your towels on the end of the bed.'

Harry straightened at the clipped words, turning to see her standing just inside the French doors, as though the last thing she wanted was to come out and join him.

His surge of irritation was acute, but he was determined not to show it. 'Thanks,' he said warmly. 'I think I'll have a shower and change into something more comfortable.'

'Fine,' she returned crisply. 'By the way, I usually serve Arnie dinner at six-thirty in the kitchen. You're quite welcome to join him, if you like lamb curry and rice. If not, then you'll have to go down to the roadhouse attached to the garage to eat. That's the only place in town

which serves meals, though I wouldn't rec-
ommend their food if you value your arteries.'

'No worries. I love lamb curry and rice.
Thanks for the offer.'

'No trouble.'

She spun on her heels and was gone in a
flash, leaving Harry wondering. Something
was bugging that girl.

But what?

Tanya bolted along the hallway and into her
room, where she shut the door and leant her
forehead against it, her hand still gripping the
knob with whitened knuckles.

She'd thought she had herself under control
where this man was concerned, that she'd rea-
soned away her earlier fluttering heart and
churning stomach with common sense logic
about hormones and the man's own devastat-
ing sex appeal.

But things were simply going from bad to
worse!

Now he didn't have to smile at her, or touch
her in any way to set her off. He only had to

be there, within reach of her traitorous eyes and even more traitorous mind.

No…she wasn't being strictly honest there. She didn't even have to be in Harry's actual physical presence for her heart to start racing and her mind to fill with disturbingly erotic thoughts about him.

What about when she'd been making up his bed?

As she'd smoothed out the sheets she hadn't been able to stop thinking about his lying there, naked, between them. He looked like the sort of man who might sleep naked.

By the time she'd actually shown him up into the bedroom she'd been in a right old state. Thank the Lord she'd had an excuse to get out of his presence before she betrayed herself by blushing.

She'd taken longer to get the towels than strictly necessary, using the time to cool herself down to some semblance of decency, only to come back and find the wretched man out there on the verandah with his jacket off and every line of his body on view for her instantly avid eyes.

Tanya groaned at the memory. There was no longer any hoping his broad shoulders were an illusion of good tailoring, or that his lower half was similarly flawed. Leaning against the railing as he had been, with those elegant grey trousers pulled tight across his backside, everything had been on open display—from his flat stomach and narrow hips to his tight, taut buttocks.

If all that hadn't been distracting enough, then there'd been the matter of the setting sun glinting golden highlights on his already sleek, shiny, please-run-your-fingers-through-my-hair head.

She'd stood and ogled him for several shameless seconds before her conscience—plus total disgust with herself—had prodded her to break the spell by speaking up and revealing her presence.

And what had he done? He'd turned round and started talking about having a shower! Naturally her imagination had wickedly taken flight once more, conjuring up images of him naked again, but this time with steamingly hot water cascading down over his beautiful male body.

She'd felt heat rising in her own body and had only just managed to escape in time.

But she couldn't stay hiding in her bedroom for ever. She had to go back downstairs soon and get on with things, or Arnie would come looking for her, wanting to know what was going on.

Tanya let go of the doorknob and began pacing round and round the room, scolding herself with strong words.

'This simply is unacceptable behaviour, Tanya,' she ground out angrily. 'He's just a man. Sydney must be full of men like him, sleek-suited success stories with smiles that curl your toes and eyes which promise too much. Once you get down there you'll see that men like him are a dime a dozen, and he'll stop affecting you this way. Familiarity does bring contempt. Till then, avoid him as much as possible. Don't look at him, or talk to him. And above all stop thinking about him! Keep busy. Keep very, very busy. You have plenty to do, after all. A meal to cook. Clothes to pack. The bar to attend to. There'll be clearing up, washing up and sweeping up. Lots to keep that wayward and wilful mind of yours occupied.'

Tanya stopped her agitated pacing and marched back to the door, determined on her new course of action.

She managed quite well too...till the wretched man came downstairs once more, shortly before six.

CHAPTER SIX

THE curried lamb was mouth-wateringly good, but the cook was nowhere in sight.

Harry had decided Tanya might have found his Armani suit intimidating—or off-putting—so he'd come downstairs at ten past six, dressed in jeans and a simple light grey sweater.

But they didn't find approval, either, if her coolly dismissive top-to-toe glance was anything to go by. He'd been promptly given a beer, then ignored till six-thirty, when he'd been bustled into the big country-style kitchen with Arnie. Once seated at the already set table, his dinner plate had been swiftly plonked in front of him, after which she'd excused herself with the speed of light.

Harry had hoped to warm her up with some flattering words about her cooking, no matter what it was like. When the curry turned out to be delicious, it annoyed him that she was no-

76

where around to accept his very genuine compliments.

'You're a lucky man,' he told Arnie instead, 'if you sit down to meals like this every night.'

'Yeah, Tanya's a great little cook. But you know what? I'm sorta lookin' forward to hamburgers and chips for a change. I'm happy to let you eat her healthy meals for a while.'

Harry was startled by this statement. 'I wouldn't *dream* of asking Tanya to cook for me whilst she's in Sydney. She'll have enough on her plate without housework. We'll eat out most nights. And when we don't, we'll just heat up some take-away in the microwave.'

Arnie guffawed. 'You won't be eating take-away while Tanya's livin' with you. Not unless you want an earful about how bad it is for your veins.'

'I think you mean arteries,' Harry corrected, privately thinking no way was anyone—least of all a female—going to lecture him about what he ate.

Arnie shrugged. 'Whatever. Just don't say I didn't warn you. Which reminds me. You don't smoke, do you?'

'Occasionally.'

'What about drink?'

'What do you mean, what about drink? Tanya already knows I drink. She just served me a beer herself. Are you saying she doesn't like men who drink?'

'Her father never knew how to stop once he started.'

'I enjoy a beer after work, and a bottle of wine with my meals.'

Another deep chuckle. 'Besta luck, then, matey.'

Harry frowned his escalating irritation. 'She doesn't sound like she's an easy person to live with.'

'Tell me about it,' Arnie grumbled.

'I gather you won't be sorry to see the back of her for a month.'

'Don't get me wrong. Tanya's a sweetie and I love her to death. But she's gettin' to that age when she needs a husband and kids of her own to mother, instead of me.'

'Well, don't start looking at *me*! I'm not going to be your saviour.'

'Hell, I already know that, Harry. But who knows? Maybe she'll meet some fella down in Sydney who'll fall in love with her and want to marry her.'

'I thought you wanted her to come back the same way she left,' Harry retorted frustratedly. 'Make up your mind, Arnie. Husband-hunting in a place like Sydney usually comes at a price, and I'm not talking about a dowry. City men don't buy without trying first these days. Best we just concentrate on securing a decent inheritance for the girl, after which I'll warrant your marriage plans for her will simply fall into place. I've always found that once a single person has some independent wealth, prospective marriage partners come leaping out of the woodwork.'

And *how*, he thought cynically. He'd been the target of fortune-hunting females more than once. What some of them would do to get a rich man's ring on their finger would make a decent girl's hair curl!

'I don't want some crummy gold-digger for her!' Arnie protested. 'I want a man who genuinely loves her.'

Harry was beginning to believe this particular twenty-three-year-old barmaid just *might* still be a virgin, especially if she'd been waiting for a non-smoking, non-drinking, only-eating-healthy-food Prince Charming to come along. Such a species was rare, and probably not given to other vices vital for deflowering, namely a normal interest in sex!

'Are you sure Tanya actually *likes* men?'

Arnie blinked surprise at this question, then laughed. 'Yeah, mate, I'm sure.'

'How sure?'

'*Very* sure.'

'Well, she sure doesn't like *me* much.'

Arnie's almost non-existent eyebrows shot ceilingwards. 'What makes you say that?'

'I can just tell. Believe me.'

Harry was slightly miffed by Arnie's amused smile. 'Bet that doesn't happen to you too often.'

'Not too often,' Harry bit out.

'Don't take it personal. Tanya's not your usual girl. Now, get on with eatin' your dinner or she'll come in and rouse on us both for lettin' it get cold.'

Harry steadily forked the rest of the delicious curry into his mouth, all the while thinking how he was going to tackle Miss Bossyboots during their month together. No way was he going to let her rule the roost as she obviously did out here. She was going to do what she was told, *when* she was told to do it. He wasn't going to take any of this so-called mothering nonsense, either. Hell, he was thirty-five years old. He didn't need a mother. What he needed was a good little obedient heiress who looked the part she was to play and performed on cue.

Unfortunately, from what he'd been hearing—and seeing for himself—Miss Tanya Wilkinson was not the most malleable of females. She *did* have a mind of her own. And a prickly, stubborn nature. Worse, she either didn't like men, or she'd had some bad experience with one which had put her off the species.

Given Arnie's assurance that the girl *was* attracted to the opposite sex, Harry opted for the latter explanation for her attitude problem.

But how to get past her cynical wariness?

Once again, his decision was to wait till he got her alone. Then he would do what he'd always done. Talk.

All women liked to talk. Especially about themselves.

Not many men actually asked women about *their* lives. They were usually too wrapped up in talking about their own ego-driven existences.

Harry never talked about himself much when he was alone with a woman. His considerable sales and social skills involved asking questions, then playing the part of interested listener. He was always amazed how, within five minutes of chatting with a female, she would start telling him her whole life story!

Harry had no doubt that given some time alone with Tanya he'd find out what really made her tick. Arnie thought he knew his little girl, but if there was one thing Harry knew for certain it was that parents, or guardians, never knew the whole story where their charges were concerned. They were not privy to all their past experiences and secret dreams. Harry, however, was an expert at uncovering both.

And then...then he would have the weaponry to get what he wanted and needed. Tanya's full co-operation.

A self-satisfied smile played around the corners of his mouth as he swallowed the last of his curry. He'd have her eating out of his hands by the time they landed at Mascot, or his name wasn't Harry Wilde!

CHAPTER SEVEN

HARRY could not believe the production they made of saying goodbye to each other the next morning. Anyone would think the infernal girl was leaving for life, not for a mere month! Hug followed hug, accompanied by a multitude of last-minute reminders and warnings.

From *both* sides.

Arnie seemed to be having second thoughts about letting his little girl go off to the big smoke in Harry's suddenly dubious company.

'You will look after her, won't you?' he asked Harry for the umpteenth time when Tanya had to dash back inside to collect something she'd apparently forgotten.

They were standing next to the blue rented Pajero. The sun was already up and promising a warmer day than winter had a right to. But that was the outback for you.

'I gave you my word,' Harry returned reproachfully, though to be honest Arnie's little girl had given him a jolt this morning when he'd first seen her.

Gone were the old ill-fitting jeans and sloppy navy sweater of the previous day, replaced by tight black ski pants, sexy black ankle boots and a soft mauve jumper which clung to her womanly curves with a disturbing degree of revelation. If the girl was wearing a bra, then her nipples had determinedly found a way through it.

He'd had to check himself when his male eyes had zeroed straight in on their highly provocative outlines.

Harry did not have a breast fetish, by any means, but erect nipples always got his libido's attention, as evidenced by the immediate prickle in his loins.

Worried that Tanya might have shifted from a *highly resistible* status to *not quite so resistible*, Harry had swiftly dragged his eyes upwards to that part of her body he found most unattractive. Her hair.

Unfortunately, she'd anchored the mass of dried-out straw back from her face with a wide black headband, covering her ginger roots and giving him a glimpse of just how attractive she could be with black hair.

She'd also made some attempt to make up her face, and, whilst it was an improvement on yesterday's *au naturel* fresh-out-of-the-midday-sun look, Harry had been almost relieved when he still found fault. Her black eyeliner was too thick and her coral lipstick all wrong.

The potential was still there, however, he mused thoughtfully, for something quite striking.

Harry immediately forgot about her perky nipples and started planning the details of her forthcoming makeover. As he envisaged the finished product in his mind's eye, his excitement level—which had waned a little overnight—zoomed back up the scale.

By God, by the time he was finished with her she'd take Femme Fatale by storm. And all who met her. Those shares were going to soar!

But to hell with her aunt's wardrobe. He wanted to see Tanya in things *he* chose for her. A thought reaffirmed when she reappeared with a cheap black gabardine jacket draped over her arm and a ghastly tapestry carryall hoisted over her shoulder. If she looked this good in such second-rate gear, then how much better would she look in designer wear, chosen especially for her by the master of image-makers—himself?

Okay, so it would cost him. But it wasn't money at stake here now, was it? Not for him, anyway. It was the challenge. Plus seeing the look on Richard's face when he pulled off mission impossible. That bottle of Grange Hermitage was as good as his right now!

'All ready to go?' he said, smiling satisfaction at her as he opened the passenger door.

She rewarded him with a look close to tears before throwing herself into Arnie's bulky arms once more.

Harry controlled his exasperation with difficulty, studying the far horizon till their final tear-filled farewell was over. Only then did he look back at Tanya, taking her arm to help her up into the passenger seat.

He gallantly resisted the temptation to openly ogle her smoothly encased and very shapely *derrière*, despite it swaying for what felt like interminable seconds before his line of vision. Nothing, however, could prevent his mind from filling with images which would have horrified Arnie. Obviously it was way past time for a night spent with Renee.

Harry didn't consider himself an over-sexed man. He could go weeks without it when he was busy at work. But when the need hit him, it hit him hard, and nothing less than a marathon session would do.

A small sigh of relief escaped his lips once Tanya was sedately seated and he was able to swing the door firmly shut on both the girl and his R-rated thoughts. Out of sight *was* out of mind, he'd often found. Men were visual creatures, after all.

'I'll give you a ring,' he promised Arnie as he shook his hand, 'as soon as we arrive in Sydney.'

'You do that. And, Harry…?'

'Yes, Arn,' he sighed. 'I'll look after her. I promise. Now, you look after yourself, hear? And watch out for the dreaded Dolly,' he added on a whisper so that Tanya didn't hear.

Arnie chuckled. 'She hasn't a hope in Hades of trappin' me, mate. I'm a confirmed bachelor from way back.'

'Famous last words,' Harry muttered as he climbed up in behind the wheel.

Tanya glanced over at him with still wet eyes. 'Did you say something?'

'Just talking to myself. All set now?'

'As set as I'll ever be,' she replied stiffly, her hands wringing a floral handkerchief to death in her lap.

He gunned the engine and backed out of the parking spot. 'If you're worried about Arnie then don't be. He's a grown man. He can look after himself.'

She snorted at this statement. 'He'll have the whisky and cigars out before our dust has settled.'

'Well, that's his prerogative as an adult, Tanya.'

With one last parting wave to the man in question, Harry put his foot down and roared out of town.

'But it's bad for his health,' his passenger persisted unhappily. 'Especially the smoking.'

'*I* smoke,' he told her bluntly.

She slanted him a startled look. 'You didn't yesterday. Or last night.'

'Actually, I did. Out on the verandah before I went to bed. But I only smoke in moderation, and only at certain times. One is when I'm driving.' And when he was suffering severe mental agitation. Last thing in the evenings. And always after sex.

'But why?' she asked, sounding truly perplexed.

'Simple reason. It relaxes me.'

Not for the first time Harry wondered why he needed to smoke after sex when the act of love was supposed to be the ultimate relaxant. He had no idea why sex never really relaxed him, but it didn't.

Driving sure didn't, either.

He reached for the cigarette packet, tapped one out and lit up, determined not to change his habits for anyone. 'You don't mind, do you?' he threw at her rather indifferently.

Her returning shrug was equally and surprisingly indifferent. 'Why should I? I'm used to smoke, having worked behind a bar so much. I watch people committing slow suicide all the time and I don't turn a hair. It's only Arnie smoking which bothers me. It's very hard to stand by and watch someone you love smoke themselves to death. But you go right ahead.'

Harry laughed, if a little ruefully. 'So tell me, Tanya,' he asked between drags on the cigarette, 'what is it about me, exactly, that you dislike so much?'

The eyes she turned on him were round with shock. 'What...what do you mean?'

'Come, now, you had it in for me from the moment I walked into the pub yesterday. So don't deny it.'

She sat there, silent, her cheeks flaming. It was so long since Harry had seen a grown woman blush that he was momentarily disarmed.

A type of guilt wormed its way into his largely desensitised soul. He really had to remember that he wasn't dealing with some tough city cookie here, but a soft-hearted country girl who was nothing at all like a typical barmaid.

'I won't be offended,' he prodded more gently at last. 'But I want the truth.'

The truth! The truth was the last thing her pride would let her tell the likes of Harry Wilde. The man was probably used to silly females swooning at his feet and forgiving him anything, even his wretched smoking.

Embarrassment twisted her stomach and scorched her face. She hadn't realised her efforts at controlling her hormones might have seemed like a case of instant dislike. But, now that Harry had pointed it out, she could see her behaviour towards him must have seemed very rude yesterday, especially when he'd come downstairs for dinner last night.

But shock that she found him even more physically attractive in casual clothes than she had in that exquisite grey suit had flustered her considerably. She'd scurried out of his sexy presence as swiftly as possible, then kept out of his way for the rest of the night.

She'd tried hard to get a grip this morning, to act naturally with the man. But she'd obviously failed. Still, what did she expect when he'd come downstairs for breakfast looking mega-gorgeous in that suit again, this time combining it with a stylish navy open-necked shirt and no tie? The mix of casual *savoir faire* and sophistication was potently attractive, setting her heart racing, her mind spinning and hands trembling.

How could she have sat with him over breakfast in that state?

She'd grabbed some toast and fled upstairs, where she'd changed her clothes several times and titivated herself as she hadn't titivated herself since Robert's departure from her life. In the end she'd come downstairs wearing a jumper which in no way matched her lipstick, but it had been too late to change everything again.

Sexual attraction, she decided, was a perverse state of affairs!

'Talk to me, Tanya,' prompted the object of her torment. But she simply did not know what to say to him.

He sighed. 'Look, we have to work closely together for the next month. If we can't communicate, then I might as well turn round and take you back home right now.'

'I don't dislike you,' she blurted out, panic-stricken at the thought he just might do that. As much as she'd dithered over leaving Arnie, she really did want to go to Sydney. And she wanted her chance to do something with her aunt's company. As daunting as that project was, it was also tremendously exciting. Almost as exciting as spending a month living and working with Harry Wilde.

'Then what's the problem?' Harry quizzed. 'Why have you been avoiding me? And why do you look at me sometimes as though I'm the devil's messenger instead of the bearer of good tidings?'

Tanya knew she had to come up with some logical explanation for her behaviour or look like a fool, which was exactly what she'd been trying to avoid.

It was just that she'd been *such* a fool over Robert. A silly, trusting, infatuated fool. She'd been absolutely hopeless from the start, wearing her naïve country heart on her sleeve and setting herself up as the perfect victim for the clever, conscienceless adulterer he'd turned out to be.

Although devastated by Robert's lies, Tanya had also been devastated to find out that her own so-called love for *him* had died a quick death once she'd been confronted by his true character. It had been a salutary lesson in life to discover she hadn't been so deeply in love after all, but suffering from a long-delayed but simple case of lust.

This time, when confronted by similar sexually driven feelings, she'd gone to the opposite extreme, keeping her distance and adopting a cold façade in the hope of protecting herself from future hurt and embarrassment.

A ridiculous precaution, really. It took two to tango, didn't it? And Harry had made it quite clear his only interest in her was professional.

'Well?' he prompted firmly.

Tanya decided that since the fiasco with Robert was to blame for her ridiculous over-reaction to Harry's sex appeal, then *he* could provide her with an excuse for her less than friendly attitude up till now.

'I'm sorry if I was rude yesterday,' she said, proud and relieved she sounded almost composed. 'I didn't realise how awful I must have seemed.' She slanted him a sincerely apologetic glance. 'The truth is you reminded me of someone I used to know…someone I didn't care to be reminded of.'

His head turned and their eyes locked. Tanya did her best to maintain her equilibrium, but his eyes really were incredible, both in their beauty and their intelligence. She could have looked into them for ever.

'A past boyfriend?' he speculated accurately.

'I guess you could describe Robert that way.'

Harry's far too intuitive gaze returned to the road ahead and Tanya's heart resumed beating.

'Mmm.'

He stubbed out the remainder of his cigarette and didn't light another. Thank heavens. As much as Tanya didn't mind the smell of smoke in a large airy room, she didn't appreciate it in the confines of a car.

'Do I look like him? Is that it?' Harry asked with another sharp sidewards glance.

'Not really…' Robert had had black wavy hair, and rather icy blue eyes which she'd thought sexy till she'd discovered the heartlessness in them. 'But he was a handsome man. Like you. And he dressed well. And he came from Sydney.'

'Ahh. I see…'

She doubted it.

'A salesman?' he asked.

'No. Some kind of efficiency expert.'

She watched him frown at that. 'What was an efficiency expert doing in Drybed Creek?'

'I didn't meet him in Drybed Creek. I met him in Broken Hill.'

His frown deepened. 'And when was that?'

'A few months ago.'

'What were you doing in Broken Hill? Shopping?'

'No, working.'

'*Working*? But I thought you worked in Arnie's pub?'

'I've only been doing that for the last couple of months. Arnie got this terrible flu virus at the beginning of winter which developed into pneumonia. I came home to look after him and the bar till he was better. I always planned to go back to Broken Hill. I've actually been living and working there since I left high school.'

'As a barmaid?'

'No. I haven't worked as a barmaid since I finished my business course. Not counting when I come home, of course.'

'So what job were you doing before you came back to Drybed Creek? Clerk? Secretary?'

'I was managing a motel.'

'*Managing* a motel?'

'Yes. Why not?' she asked, piqued a little by his ongoing surprise.

'I was told you were a barmaid,' he replied.

'Sorry to disillusion you.'

'I'm not disillusioned. I'm impressed. I assume the boyfriend from Sydney stayed at this motel of yours?'

'He did. For a while…' Three weeks and one day, to be precise.

'And was it serious between you two?'

'I thought so at the time.'

'So what happened?'

'There was a fire at the motel one night, and one whole wing burned down. A man died of smoke inhalation. It made the Sydney news and the next morning Robert's wife rang up in a panic to see if her beloved was okay.'

'Oh-oh.'

'Yes, oh-oh,' she repeated grimly.

'So what did you do?'

'I told him to find another motel to stay at and another fool to lie to.'

'And?'

'He went.' Not straight away, but eventually. In the beginning he had insisted he really did love her, but he couldn't leave his wife because of the children. He'd claimed he hadn't told her the truth because he'd known she wouldn't have anything to do with him if he knew he was married.

He'd been right.

Poor kid, Harry thought, as he noted her twisting hands and tightly held mouth.

It always angered him when men lied to girls like Tanya to get sex. It was low, and just so unnecessary! There were plenty of liberated females out there willing to give men whatever they wanted these days, without strings, and certainly without lies.

But some men seemed compelled to go for the naïve, innocent ones, sweet, soft girls who really couldn't handle a sexual relationship without love and some kind of commitment. So these creeps told their quarries they loved them. Promised them the world. Played games with their emotions. All with the sole purpose of getting them into bed.

Why? Harry puzzled. Because they had a fetish for virgin flesh? Because they were just plain bad bastards who liked the challenge of tearing down old-fashioned virtue? Or was it because they were inadequate lovers who felt safer with inexperienced girls because that way their partners had nothing to compare their pathetic performance with?

Who knew?

Harry didn't. All he new was he despised the type.

Still, in the light of what he'd just learnt, and the girl's reactions, Harry now believed that she *had* been a virgin till she'd met this smooth-talking seducer from Sydney.

But she sure as hell wasn't now. She wouldn't be so bitter about this Robert character if she hadn't slept with him. And more than once.

'You know, not all men from Sydney are like that,' he pointed out gently.

'Well, I wouldn't know,' she retorted, her face turned away from him. 'I've only ever been involved with one.'

'How old was he?'

'I don't know,' she said, turning back to face him. 'I never actually asked. He looked about your age. How old are you?'

'Thirty-five.'

'You look younger.'

'Thanks.'

'Obviously the smoking hasn't caught up with you,' she said, then added drily, 'Yet.'

He laughed. 'Neither have the take-away food, wine or wild, wild women.'

'Wild, wild women?' she repeated with widening eyes.

Yep, he thought. An innocent, till *el creepo* came along. He would have to be careful not to shock her too much. At the same time he wasn't about to put his life on hold, or to pretend he was something he wasn't.

'In truth, there aren't too many of those these days,' he said, 'and only ever one at a time. But I thought I'd better acquaint you with all of my vices up-front before we start living together. The fact is, Tanya, I occasionally have a lady-friend stay the night. I hope that won't be a problem. Naturally I will be discreet, with all activities confined to the master bedroom, which is quite removed from the guest suite you'll be occupying.'

There was disapproval in the sudden squaring of her shoulders and the way she pressed her spine back into the passenger seat. But Harry had no intention of backing down, or compromising on this.

'I want it understood right from the start,' he stated firmly, 'that I won't be changing my normal lifestyle just because you're staying with me.'

'I wouldn't expect you to,' she agreed, if somewhat stiffly.

'Good. Now that we've got that straight, is there anything you want to tell me about yourself? Any special needs *you* might have, or anything you simply can't do without? Arnie said you liked to cook and eat healthily. I did tell him we'd be eating out together most nights, but—'

'Just the two of us, you mean?' she broke in.

'You have a problem with that?'

'No, no, it's just that…well, what about your girlfriend?'

'Renee and I don't live in each other's pockets. I rarely see her more than once a week, and never on a week night. Now, about your passion for healthy eating… Let me assure you that the restaurants I frequent will happily prepare anything you want the way you want it. Still, if you'd ever rather stay in and cook yourself something, you only have to say so. Though I might have to get some groceries in first. I really don't keep much in the way of food supplies at home, since I don't cook.'

'You don't cook at *all*? *Ever*?'

'Never.'

'What about your girlfriend?'

Harry laughed. 'Good God, no. Renee doesn't cook, either. She's a PR executive for an airline and barely has time to eat, let alone cook.'

Mentioning Renee's job reminded Harry that she was the exception when it came to his usual choice of girlfriend. He'd only given in to the temptation to date such a super-smart female after he'd realised she was married to her job.

Still, he didn't like the vibes he'd been getting from Renee lately. The snide remarks about how little time he actually spent with her. She'd been hinting about their going away somewhere for a whole weekend together.

Harry never spent the whole weekend with a woman. That always gave them ideas. Even the dumb ones.

'What about breakfast?' Tanya asked, sounding genuinely bewildered. She was looking over at him, her quite lovely eyes big with wonder.

Harry promptly forgot about Renee. 'I don't have breakfast at home,' he told her. 'On a weekday I get coffee and a bagel when I arrive at work. At the weekends I sleep late, then just drink coffee till it's time to get dressed and go out for lunch.'

'You go out to lunch *every* day?' Her tone was disbelieving. So was her face.

'Most days. During the week I have lots of business lunches, though there *is* the odd day I have sandwiches brought in from a local deli.'

'And you eat out every night as well?'

'Again, mostly. On the nights I don't dine out I bring home take-away. Or have something delivered.'

'That must be a very expensive way to live.'

'I guess it is. But I can afford it.' Wait till she saw his fully serviced penthouse.

Harry had a distinct aversion to any kind of work around the house. Probably because he'd been forced to do so much of it during his growing up years. His aunt had been a lazy slob who'd made him do everything she should have done. All the cooking and cleaning, as well as the yard work. He'd been an unpaid slave from the age of eight to sixteen.

Now, he never lifted a finger to do anything at home. A woman came in every week for a couple of hours to tidy and clean the place, leaving it spotless for his return that evening. She also looked after his clothes, taking his suits to the dry-cleaners and his shirts to a professional laundry. The rest she popped into the washer and dryer whilst she was there. Every Friday she stayed longer, to do any ironing or special jobs. A professional window cleaner looked after the windows, and twice a year carpet cleaners were brought in to bring the expensive shag-pile carpet back to its velvety plush best.

'You must be very rich,' Tanya said in a quietly thoughtful voice.

'I am.' Modesty was not Harry's strong point.

She fell silent at this juncture, and Harry wondered what she was thinking. Probably that he was arrogant and extravagant and totally selfish in the way he lived his life.

If he was, he'd earned the right, in his opinion. He'd worked his backside off for years and taken risks not many men would have taken. Now he was enjoying the fruits of his labour to the full, and to hell with anyone who looked down on him for that.

Still, he was beginning to feel a tad piqued by her ongoing silence. Then she looked over at him with a totally unreadable expression.

'Tell me about my aunt,' she said abruptly, 'and why my father said she was wicked.'

CHAPTER EIGHT

THE change of subject was desperation tactics on Tanya's part. Although naturally curious about her aunt, she was driven more by a need to distract herself from thoughts about this man and his decadent lifestyle!

She could not stand the visions which kept filling her head, or the jabs of jealousy which accompanied images of him and his girlfriend cavorting all night in his bedroom whilst she would be lying in her lonely bed, craving the man even more than she'd craved Robert.

The master bedroom, Harry had called it.

There was no doubt in Tanya's mind that he'd be master there too, this man who was so sure of himself in every facet in his life.

When Harry had asked her to tell him of any needs she might have that she simply could not do without, she'd wanted to cry out, *Just you!*

But wanting Harry Wilde was a foolish and futile female fantasy, and one which Tanya refused to indulge in any longer!

Which was why she'd asked him about her aunt.

'I'm not sure why your father called Maxine wicked,' Harry replied, relieved that the conversation had turned away from himself. 'I don't know what would constitute wicked in his mind. Was he a religious man?'

'Not really.'

'What was his attitude to sex?'

'He never talked to me about sex. It wasn't a part of his life after my mother died, so it never came up and I never asked.'

'Tell me about your mother,' Harry asked, and reached for another cigarette.

'What? Oh. Oh, well, there's not much to tell. Or should I say there's not much I know. She died when I was eighteen months old, so I have no personal recollection of her. I don't have any photos, either. Dad rarely spoke of her. Arnie finally told me a few facts after

Dad's death, which filled in a few of the gaps. I was curious, as you can imagine.'

Harry was too, so much so that the cigarette went back into the packet, unlit.

'So what did Arnie tell you about her?'

'Nothing complimentary. She was a tart, pure and simple. A good-time girl who'd gone to the opal fields of Coober Pedy to make her fortune the way good-time girls have been making it for centuries. She bed-hopped from miner to miner, depending on how their stake was going at the time. When my father hit town and struck it lucky she latched onto him for a while. When his lucky streak ran out, she left him for another fellow and he went bush. When he came back a couple of years later to look her up, he found out she'd had a kid. Me.

'According to Arnie, Dad said he knew I was his straight away because I was the dead spit of his sister when she was a toddler. Dad also told him that my mother was the only woman who ever got to him, sexually speaking. Who knows? Maybe he was really in love with her. He'd told Arnie she was…incredible…that way. She could make whatever man she was with feel ten feet tall. Whatever, he certainly never looked at another one in all the years I was with him.'

'How did your Dad get custody of you?'

'When he found me, my mum had just died. Of snake bite, would you believe? A king brown. Anyway, another woman was looking after me and didn't want to let me go. Luckily my mother had put Dad's name down on my birth certificate, so once Dad proved who he was she had to let him take me. Which is why I talk with a funny accent. Dad was from England, you see.'

'Yes, I know. It was in the investigator's report.'

'We went everywhere together. We were great mates and he was a good father in his own peculiar way. Not that he changed his ways for me. I had to fit right in with whatever he wanted to do. We never had a proper home, camping out most of the time.'

'So how did you come to be at Arnie's pub?'

'Dad came to that area when I was eight. Back in those days Drybed Creek was a thriving little town. The local mine was rich with tin and silver and copper. Anyway, Dad stayed there for a while and became good friends with Arnie. Dad made friends with the hotel owner in whatever town we were in. He was a heavy drinker, was Dad. Arnie, however, took a real shine to me. He told Dad I should have a more settled life and be sent to school. He nagged at Dad till he agreed to take me along to the local teacher, who threatened to dob Dad in to the authorities if he didn't see to my education quick-smart. The upshot was Dad rented a couple of rooms from Arnie on a semi-permanent basis and my more traditional life began, with Arnie looking after me whenever Dad was away.'

'A most unusual existence,' Harry remarked. 'And one which other authorities might still have frowned upon.'

'I know what you mean, but truly I was well looked after. The whole town had taken me under their wing. Not just Arnie. And the country is not like the city. Bad things don't happen to kids in the outback.'

'You reckon? I know one kid who didn't fare too well in the bloody outback.'

Harry regretted the bitter words the moment they were out of his mouth, for they sent Tanya's head rocketing round with a stunned look in her eyes.

'You come from the outback? I don't believe it!'

'I lived on a remote cattle station in Queensland from the age of eight to sixteen,' he admitted ruefully. 'Not with my parents. My mother died when I was five. My father had already done a flit and couldn't be located. I was put in a state-run home in Brisbane till my aunt and uncle kindly decided to give me a home.'

'You didn't like life on a cattle station?' she asked, sounding genuinely surprised.

'Let's just say I would have preferred to stay in the state-run home, and *it* was pretty appalling.'

'Oh. How sad for you. As much as I'm not that keen on living out here now, I had a very happy childhood. I can't understand why you found living in the outback so bad. Most boys love it. Though of course you weren't born to it like the ones I know. Was it the weather? The remoteness? What?'

Harry had to check himself, because the temptation to tell her everything was absurdly acute. Perhaps because she seemed so genuinely interested.

But he'd never told another living soul about the details of those hellish years and he didn't aim to start now. There was nothing to be gained from wallowing in the past, he believed. Such drivel made you weak. And overly emotional. It was okay for a woman, but not for a man.

What good could it possibly do to talk about the past, anyway? It was the present which mattered. And the future.

And the future was what Tanya had asked him to tell her about. Her aunt. Somehow they'd got right off track, and it was up to him to put them right back.

'The past is the past,' he said brusquely. 'No point raking it up. Now, you were asking about your aunt and why your father might have called her wicked. Look, it might have been because she made her living selling lingerie. Frankly, some of Femme Fatale's stuff is *very* sexy. But I suspect it was because she was a lesbian.'

Shock pulled Tanya back from her curiosity about Harry's childhood.

'A lesbian!' she exclaimed.

'The woman who was killed in the car accident with her wasn't just Femme Fatale's marketing manager. She was Maxine's lover. Maxine had, in fact, left her estate to this woman. But because she pre-deceased her the estate then went to you.'

'Heavens! How amazing! I don't know what to say. Did everyone at the company know about their relationship?'

'I certainly did. Maxine didn't flaunt her sexuality, but she didn't hide it, either. Why? Do you have some problem with your aunt being a lesbian?'

'Not really. It's a bit of a shock, though. I hope the staff at Femme Fatale don't think I'm a chip off the old block.'

'I doubt it,' Harry said drily. 'Not with me glued to your side.'

Tanya swallowed at the thought of Harry glued to her side, day in and day out. How was she going to stand it? 'You mean they…they'll think we're lovers?'

'Possibly. Will that bother you?'

'Not if it doesn't bother you,' she returned carefully. 'But what will Renee think?'

'Renee won't think a thing.'

Tanya was truly shocked. 'She lets you sleep with other women?'

'She doesn't *let* me do anything,' he returned quite sharply. 'I do as I please.'

Tanya didn't know what to say, or think.

Arnie had said Harry was a lad with the ladies. Clearly that was an understatement. He was a playboy of the worst kind, his only saving grace being that he was honest about it. Okay, so he was a cut above Robert, in that he didn't break sacred vows or lie to get a woman into bed. He didn't need to. He just took what he wanted when he wanted it.

Which should have made him less attractive to her.

But it didn't! Not in the slightest. If anything, Tanya found him even more fascinating.

She couldn't even accuse him of being shal-
low, because he wasn't. In truth, he was prov-
ing to be a very complex man, with a myste-
rious past which she could only guess at.
Using female intuition, she guessed that love
hadn't come into his upbringing too much,
judging by the scars he still carried.

But did that excuse him callously using a
woman for his own carnal ends without caring
about her feelings?

'Naturally I will tell Renee that there is
nothing between us,' he added firmly, before
she began to worry that he was beyond re-
demption.

'Will she believe you?' Tanya had a feeling
if *she* was Harry's girlfriend she might not.

'But of course. I told you. I have never lied
to the women in my life. And they know it.'

'They?'

He smiled a wickedly knowing smile.
'There have been quite a few. I admit.'

'But only one at a time these days, you
said,' she reminded him drily.

'You sound sceptical.'

'No. Just trying to understand you.'

He laughed. 'Now there's a tall order. Don't try to understand me, Tanya. Not in one short month. Just do as I say and with a bit of luck you'll come out of this with more money than you've ever dreamed of. You'll be able to *buy* that motel when you go back to Broken Hill.'

CHAPTER NINE

'Oh, look! I can see Sydney. Oh, my goodness, it's so huge! Golly, I've never seen so many roofs in my life. Or so many swimming pools! Oh, and there's the sea. And the beaches. And the sand. I've never been to a beach before. Oh, the water's so blue and so beautiful. And I think I can see the harbour. Harry, lean over and look. Can you see it? Straight down there!'

Tanya's excitement took Harry back to his own feelings on first sighting Sydney, though that hadn't been from up in the sky. He'd been in the cab of a removalist's van, having hitch-hiked all the way from the far north west of Queensland. He'd been dirty and dusty and dead tired, but he'd still been captivated by the city. From his position high up in the truck's passenger seat he'd been able to see over the railings of the bridge, and the sight of Sydney Harbour on a bright summer's day had blown him away. The blueness. The boats. But above all the sheer, stunning beauty of it all.

The seeds of ambition had been sown at that moment. One day, he'd vowed, he would be rich enough to own a place right on that harbour.

It had taken over a decade of slogging his guts out, but he'd finally achieved his goal.

'No, that's not Port Jackson,' he said, having unclipped his seatbelt to lean over her and look at where she was pointing. 'That's Botany Bay. Sydney Harbour and the bridge are further north. You probably can't see it from this angle. But no worries, you'll see it all to absolute perfection from my place.'

She turned her head and their noses brushed, whereupon she gave a little gasp and her eyes jerked up to his: wide, violet eyes which were still dancing with delight at what she'd just seen.

Harry should have drawn back into his own seat, he supposed. But he didn't. He stayed right where he was, beseiged by the most unwise urge to kiss her, to taste some of that child-like pleasure which had been enchanting

him since they'd arrived at Broken Hill airport
and she'd confessed to never having flown before.

Everything about the flight had thrilled her.
The first-class seats and service. The take-off.
The champagne. The food. And now their destination. All of a sudden he ached to sip at the
cup of her sweetness, to drink in some of her
first-time pleasure, to share her experience of
wonder and joy. Just observing her excitement
was not enough. He wanted to feel it for himself, up close and personally.

He might have too, if the steward hadn't
materialised at his shoulder that very second,
stating that they'd already started their descent
into Mascot and would he please refasten his
seatbelt.

Saved from the moment of madness, Harry
slumped gratefully back into his seat and
snapped the belt into place.

But he remained perturbed that he'd almost
given in to such a stupid impulse. Kissing
Tanya would have really mucked up his mission. Girls didn't appreciate men groping them
out of the blue these days. Certainly not girls

like Tanya. She would probably have decided he was a lech, like that Robert fellow, then taken the next flight back to Broken Hill.

Harry dragged in a deep, slightly ragged breath, then let it out slowly, carefully. Hell, that had been close. Too close for comfort.

He couldn't remember the last time he'd almost acted so foolishly with a female. There wouldn't be any steward to rescue him once he had her all alone in his penthouse, either. All he would have then was his own common sense and sexual self-control, which seemed to be sadly lacking at the moment.

Nothing a night with Renee won't fix up, his cynical side reminded him. *Call the woman as soon as you land and line her up for tonight.*

Harry mentally shook his head. No, not tonight. It would be too rude to leave Tanya alone the first night she arrived in Sydney. He really should take her out somewhere special, show her the sights of the city. Not much danger of anything happening in public. He'd book a table at The Quay, one of his favourite restaurants.

It shouldn't be too busy on a Wednesday night at this time of year. With a bit of luck he might even get one of the best tables with the best views. There was no trouble with parking there, either. Renee would have to wait till Friday night. That suited her best, anyway. She'd be too tired for what he had in mind on a week night. Far too tired.

Glancing over at the girl who was unconsciously causing him all these problems, Harry was startled to see she was gripping the sides of her seats with white-knuckled ferocity. Admittedly, the plane was banking rather severely over the sea. Not a comfortable experience for a first-time flyer. For one thing the wingtips always looked much closer to the water than they actually were.

Poor thing, he thought. She looked frightened to death. And very young. Very, *very* young, he reminded himself ruefully.

Remembering his promise to Arnie to look after his little girl, he reached out and covered her nearest hand with his. Her violet eyes shot round to his, wide and full of fear. His hand exerted a gentle pressure on hers in a reassuring gesture.

'Don't worry,' he said softly. 'This is normal procedure. We're not going to crash. Everything is going to be all right.'

And he actually believed it would be.

Tanya almost laughed. He had no idea. Simply no idea. Otherwise he wouldn't be doing what he was doing and plummeting her back into Panicsville.

Clearly he thought she was worried about the plane landing. But nothing was further from her mind—not since he'd leant over her a minute or two ago. Bad enough when his face had been so close to hers, their eyes locked and their breath mingling. Worse now that he was actually touching her, his hand curved intimately over hers, his palm warm and smooth, his fingers squeezing hers with what he no doubt thought was a comforting gesture.

Oh, God…

She'd done really well all through the flight, ignoring the dizzying pleasure she felt just being with this man and pretending it wasn't his company thrilling her but everything else.

'We'll be safely down soon,' he added, giving her stiffened hand a final pat before thankfully lifting his away.

But the memory of its touch lingered, as did the heat his hand had engendered in her own, and all through her body.

Tanya tried to remember if things had been this inflammatory with Robert. She didn't think so, although the chemistry must have been strong to have propelled her into his motel room in three short weeks, ready and eager to sleep with him; a momentous step for a girl who'd vowed not to sleep with any man till she was at least engaged to him.

She'd been so smug about her virtue up till that point, not realising how effortless it was to be pure when your flesh wasn't screaming at you to be otherwise.

Of course, she'd told herself that she and Robert were madly in love. Just an excuse, really, a justification for her actions. The truth was she'd simply been overwhelmed by the addictive pleasure of Robert's kisses, and the promise of more pleasure to come. It worried her sometimes what might have happened if she hadn't found out he was married till *after* she'd slept with him.

Maybe she was more like her mother than she'd ever realised. Maybe she'd just needed a certain type of man to bring out the good-time girl in her. Maybe all successful, sophisticated men in Italian suits turned her on, then into this creature who craved their touch, and their bodies.

It was a worrying thought, given she was about to land in a city where such men would not be a rarity. Would her head be turned at every corner? Would she be slavering over them *all*?

It wasn't till the plane had safely landed and she was moving through the huge terminal with Harry by her side that *this* fear began to subside.

Because the place was full of stylish men in superb suits, striding along with mobile phones clamped to their ears and designer briefcases by their sides.

Several of them glanced at her as they went by, making eye contact, but not one did a thing for her. She felt nothing like the way she felt when Harry looked at her. Tanya almost sighed with relief. Better she be enslaved by one unwise infatuation than be madly attracted, willy-nilly, to every good-looking suit she encountered.

'Feeling better now that your feet are on the ground?' Harry asked as they stepped off the escalator which had carried them down to ground level.

Tanya let out the breath she'd been unconsciously holding. 'Much better, thanks,' she said, her mind now settled enough to enjoy her arrival in the city of her dreams.

Initially, Sydney was not quite what she'd expected, the taxi ride first taking them through some grim and grey-looking streets. There was certainly nothing of any beauty to behold.

'Don't judge Sydney by the area around the airport,' Harry told her, perhaps when he saw the look on her face. 'It's mostly industrial areas from here, almost to the city centre.

Unfortunately we'll be skirting the city centre as well today, and heading straight across the harbour to the north side, and home. The CBD, though exciting, is a place best avoided in a car in the daytime. They're always tearing things down and building something new, blocking off roads and causing havoc in general. But that's progress. Sydney's a young city, always changing, always growing. I love that about it, actually. Still, it's not everyone's cup of tea. Too hectic and noisy, sometimes, even for Sydneysiders.'

'I don't mind the noise so much,' Tanya said truthfully. 'I just never knew there were so many cars in the *world*, let alone Australia.'

Suddenly, in the distance, she spied what had to be the city centre skyline: office blocks and towers stretching up unbelievably high, most of them with huge signs sitting on top.

It looked spectacular!

Now *this* was what she'd been waiting for, and her heart was racing with anticipation as they drew closer and her eyes lifted higher and higher. The taxi picked up speed and everything seemed to be rushing past far too quickly for her to take it all in. When the taxi suddenly zoomed into a tunnel, Tanya groaned her disappointment.

'Unfortunately this road goes into the harbour tunnel and not over the bridge,' Harry said. 'But, to be honest, you can't see all that much from car level on the bridge. We'll walk over it some time soon. We could even climb it, if you're game. I'll take you on a harbour cruise too, if you'd like.'

'If I'd *like*!' she exclaimed, perhaps too breathlessly. But it made her breathless, sitting this close to him in the back seat of a car, especially when she swung her knees around his way and their thighs brushed.

'It would be my pleasure,' he returned with seeming sincerity. 'I love showing Sydney off to visitors. I have a feeling I would especially love showing it off to you.'

'Oh? Why me especially?' she couldn't resist asking as her heart fluttered madly.

'Because you remind me so much of myself when I first came here. I too found it incredible after living in the outback.'

At that moment they burst out of the tunnel, and Tanya twisted round to stare back up at the bridge behind her, with its huge pylons and spectacular coathanger shape. The size of the structure was awesome to a girl from the bush.

'It *is* pretty incredible, isn't it?' she said.

'I think so. I would never want to live anywhere else. Wait till you see the view from my place,' he finished proudly.

'I have a feeling,' she said as she turned back round to look at him, 'that your place is not some simple two-bedroomed flat with a tiny balcony and an even tinier glimpse of water in the distance.'

He laughed. 'Not quite.'

'It's a palace of a place, right?'

'A fairly large penthouse. Yes.'

A penthouse for a playboy, she thought. With the occasional penthouse pet brought in for his amusement. The thought should have disgusted her, but she was consumed with a corrupting envy. What would she not give to be his penthouse pet, if only for a night?

'How many bedrooms?' she asked thickly.

'Four.'

'Er...how big's the balcony?'

'It's of the wraparound kind. There's a three-hundred-and-sixty-degree view.'

She gaped. 'You mean you own the whole floor?'

'Uh-huh.'

'Good grief, you must be a multimillion-aire!'

'I told you I was rich.'

'I didn't realise just *how* rich.'

'Does it matter? At least my wealth means I'm not trying to make any money for myself out of this. You don't have to distrust my motives in bringing you to Sydney.'

'But I *don't* distrust your motives. Not any more, anway. I would never have come with you if I did.'

His smile was wry. 'You mean you'd have turned your back on the chance of all that lovely money?'

'No. I'd have contacted the firm of solicitors who are handling my aunt's estate and made my own arrangements,' she said firmly. 'I don't let anybody run my life or make my decisions for me unless I'm in agreement with them.'

'Sensible girl,' he said, nodding. 'Actually, I had a feeling from the first moment I met you that you weren't going to be easily persuaded. I hope, however, that you can take advice.'

'What kind of advice?'

'About the image I have planned for you.'

'What kind of image?'

The taxi interrupted their conversation by arriving at their destination, having woven its way down some narrow side-streets lined with parked cars.

'Tell you when we get upstairs,' Harry said, and reached for the taxi door. Tanya did the same on her side, alighting onto a concrete pavement outside a very modern-looking apartment block. The water was nowhere in sight, but she suspected it lay the other side of the buildings which lined the *cul-de-sac*, since they hadn't travelled all that far from the harbour bridge.

Harry's building stretched up for at least a dozen floors. Probably more. A blue glass and

grey concrete structure, it had recessed balco-
nies which didn't spoil the square shape, and
a spacious glassed-in foyer complete with a security desk and security guard which would
have done the White House proud.

Harry used what looked like a bank card to
gain entrance through the heavy glass door, in-
serting it into a weird lock before a green light
came on and the door could be pushed open.
After exchanging greetings with the burly security guard, whose name was Fred, Harry introduced Tanya as his house-guest for the next
month and requested a pass key card for her
personal use. Fred duly supplied one, after
which Harry picked up the luggage again and
led a gog-eyed Tanya into a waiting lift, where
he instructed her how to use her card to operate
the lift as well.

Tanya managed after two botched attempts,
for the procedure was foreign to her personal
experience. She'd seen such things in
American movies but had had no idea they
were standard security procedure in Sydney.

'There's nothing like this out at Broken
Hill,' she said on their ride up to the penthouse

floor. 'Or if there is I've never come across it. Isn't it a little excessive for a residential block?'

'Stops robberies,' Harry said succinctly. 'And unwanted guests arriving at your door.' The lift doors whooshed open. 'You go first.' He indicated with a nod, following her into a large foyer with their luggage. Her heels made a clacking noise on the marble floor.

'What if it's a wanted guest?' she asked, while Harry dropped the luggage at the large cream-painted door in front of them. Matching marble hall-tables with gilt legs were set on either side of the door, their elegantly shaped mirrors ready for any last-second primping by female visitors such as the much envied Renee.

'People can buzz an apartment from outside the front door and be let in that way,' Harry replied as he fished for his keys in his trouser pocket. 'Then the security guard escorts them to the lift, where he uses his card to let them come up.'

'How do they get down again?'

'You only need the card to go up, not go down.'

'What if you lose your card?'

'All the security guards make it their business to know all the residents and their houseguests. Whoever's on duty will always let you in, then give you another card. But try not to lose it. And keep a close eye on your bag when you're out. Sydney's a beautiful city, but it's still a city with all the risks a city collects.'

'I'll be careful,' she said firmly. 'And I won't lose my card. I'm a very careful person.'

'That's good,' he said. 'You'll need to be.'

Tanya heard the wry tone and wondered if he was implying she would be like a babe in the woods here in Sydney? If he thought that, then he was mistaken. She might be a country hick compared to him, but, generally speaking, she could look after herself. She'd been living alone for quite a few years, supporting herself, being responsible for herself.

Broken Hill might not be Sydney but it was a far cry from Drybed Creek. And not lilywhite by any means. She'd had to handle all sorts of sticky situations in her job managing the motel there. And all sorts of men. Drunks.

Sleazy salesmen on the make. Pushy macho guys who didn't like to take no for an answer.

Okay, so Robert had turned her into a temporary fool with his smooth good looks and even smoother lies. But on a practical day-to-day basis Tanya had every confidence in herself as a survivor. She was not a girl who needed a minder. Or a chaperon, for that matter!

So isn't it time you started acting like it? mocked a caustic inner voice.

'I can look after myself, you know,' she said, almost defensively. 'I'm twenty-three years old.'

'Twenty-three seems quite young to me,' Harry returned as he slipped a key into the deadlock.

'Girls mature more quickly than boys,' she pointed out, holding back her anger with difficulty. He really could be horribly patronising!

'I have no doubt about that. I'm sure you're a very mature girl, compared to a boy of the same age.'

'I'm a woman, not a girl.'

His glance over his shoulder at her was de-cidedly sardonic, as though her idea of what a woman constituted was different from his. She did her best not to blush, but failed abysmally.

'In that case,' he said wryly whilst he threw open the door and flourished his right hand across his body in a mock wave, 'come into my parlour…woman.'

CHAPTER TEN

HARRY watched her chin lift defiantly, even while her cheeks went bright red. She stalked confidently past him into the penthouse, oblivious to what he could do to her if he ever chose to ignore the promises he'd made to Arnie. She would have no real defences against his experience, and his knowledge of women. All her so-called strength of character would be as nothing if he set his mind to a merciless seduction.

Her naïvety both frustrated and enchanted him. Hell, she didn't even know how to operate a keycard! How long had it been since he'd brought a woman up here who hadn't tasted everything life—and men—had to offer? And he meant *everything*!

Tanya, however, was a relative innocent. She might not be a virgin any more, but she was still very inexperienced. Why else would she blush at the drop of a hat?

The truth was she'd probably only gone to bed with *el creepo* a couple of times. Even then, his performance had probably been pathetic.

It stirred Harry to think of all the things he could show her, and the pleasure he could give her. Too bad his thoughts would never become reality.

Harry had always been a man of his word. And he'd given it to Arnie. Okay, so sleeping with Tanya wouldn't technically be breaking his promise about bringing her back to Drybed Creek the same way she'd left, since she wasn't a virgin after all. But he couldn't in all conscience convince himself that seducing the girl was looking after her.

Different if she'd been a bit older, and less vulnerable. The trouble with a girl like Tanya was that she would think herself in love with him before he could say, *Pass me another condom, darling.*

So, no…there would be no merciless seduction here tonight. Or any other night during the coming month. He wasn't about to sink *that* low.

But, by God, she was a temptation. More than he'd ever imagined when he'd first met her.

Battening down his frustration with an iron will, Harry brought in the luggage and locked the door behind him.

'Right,' he said brusquely as he turned to face her once more. 'A quick tour of the place, then I have to make some important phone calls and get this show on the road.'

Tanya trailed after a briskly striding Harry, her eyes widening at what unfolded before her eyes. Expecting a palace of a place had been one thing, but seeing it first-hand was a mind-blowing experience.

It wasn't the luxury of the furniture and furnishings which stunned her so much as the size. Everything was so large. The living rooms—and there were several. The kitchen. The bathrooms. The bedrooms.

Tanya could not believe the room Harry said she would be sleeping in. The bed was huge, with the most beautiful bedspread in green silk shot with silver.

The master bedroom—and bed—seemed even bigger, decorated in blues and greys, with pale grey furniture. The adjoining bathroom was fit for a king, wall-to-wall streaky grey marble, silver fittings, and a crystal chandelier in the ceiling.

She oohed and aahed in awe at everything inside, but it was the outdoor areas which left her speechless. The word 'balcony' was totally inadequate to describe the wide terracotta-tiled terraces which encompassed the penthouse.

As for the view…

Tanya stood transfixed by the sight of the harbour and the city beyond, its striking sky-line both softened and enhanced by the late-afternoon light. The bridge was to her right, the water below it a midnight-blue, its surface calm, a marvelous mirror for the lights which were beginning to wink on all over the place. The Opera House was straight across, in its perfect setting on Bennelong Point, the famous sail roofs looking every bit as spectacular as they did in photos. Between the Opera House and the bridge lay Circular Quay, where the many harbour ferries deposited and picked up passengers.

Tanya watched a ferry go by below her, not all that far away from the shoreline. She peered down at the people leaning on the railings, their faces lifted as though looking back up at her.

What a way to go home at the end of the day, she thought, and decided then and there she would never go back to Broken Hill. This was the life for her. Here, in this big, bustling, beautiful city!

Whatever happened with Femme Fatale, she would stay.

'So, what do you think?' Harry asked by her side.

She sighed. 'You are so lucky to live here, Harry.'

'Luck didn't have much to do with it,' he said rather sharply. 'Now, shall we go ring Arnie and let him know you've arrived safe and sound?'

'Oh, yes. Please.'

She followed him through the nearest sliding glass door and across the thick velvety green carpet which covered all the living area floors out into the main central hallway and in through another door which Harry had briefly opened earlier. Behind it lay a study-cum-library-cum-reading room. Huge, as usual, and eclectic in decor, as was the rest of the penthouse.

A cool leather sofa in pale blue sat alongside two rich grey and silver brocade chairs, all grouped around a low glass coffee table in front of an elegantly carved fireplace. On the opposite side of the room a brown leather studded chair with armrests sat behind a long polished mahogany desk, behind which stretched a wall lined with glass shelves and filled from ceiling to floor with books. Modern recessed light fittings dotted the ceiling, yet the standing lamps dotted around the room were brass-based, their pale green shades fringed the old-fashioned way.

Surprisingly, the mix of colours, styles and textures didn't look at all odd. In fact it worked amazingly well. When Tanya had asked Harry if he'd chosen everything himself, his answer had been short and sweet.

'Good Lord, no. The place came fully furnished.'

He'd dropped any pretence of polite small talk since arriving, adopting a far more businesslike attitude than he had on the drive to Broken Hill and during the flight to Sydney. Clearly he was back in city mode, a busy businessman with things to do. She wondered when she could politely ask him about this new image he had in mind for her.

He didn't sit in the chair behind the desk, just swept the receiver off its cradle and perched himself up on a corner, his eyes meeting hers matter-of-factly as he punched in a number. 'Just ringing a restaurant for tonight first,' he told her.

'Oh, no, please, Harry, not tonight,' she blurted out. 'I...I'm a bit tired, and honestly I don't want to go anywhere till my hair is fixed.' She'd tried to forget about it all day— and had managed to a degree—but seeing the beauty of Harry's penthouse had reminded her of her own physical inadequacies.

'But you go of course,' she swept on, before he could do more than frown. 'I...I'll just have toast or something. Look, I know it's vain of me, but I simply hate looking this way.'

He shrugged. 'Fair enough. I'll order something in. What's Arnie's number?' he asked, and she told him.

He dialled, then waited.

'Arnie?' he said at last. 'Harry. Yes, we're here at my place...' A small laugh. 'No, the plane didn't crash, though I think Tanya was worried there for a moment during our descent into Mascot... Yes, she's right here, ready and eager to talk to you. Just a sec.' Harry beckoned her over. 'Talk as long as you like,' he offered as he handed her the receiver. 'I have a couple of private calls to make. I have another line in my bedroom. Be back shortly.'

Harry was glad to leave her to it and glad to be finally doing something about lining up Renee for a night of sex and sin. That girl was definitely getting under his skin.

Her bringing his attention back to her hair had been a real eye-opener. The disturbing truth was he'd begun not to really see it. Just those big violet eyes of hers, those big beautiful, beckoning eyes.

Harry slammed into his bedroom, muttering his irritation out loud.

'I'll have her damn hair cut short. That's what I'll do. I hate short hair on a woman. And I'll forget that stupid idea of dressing her personally in clothes I like. Let her wear Maxine's clothes!'

Harry marched over to the side of his king-sized bed and snatched up the phone, punching in Renee's work number with swift sharp jabs. She'd still be in her office. She never left it till seven at the earliest on a week night.

She answered on the second ring. 'Renee Harley,' she said in that slightly husky, rather knowing voice he'd always thought incredibly sexy. Why, then, was he suddenly preferring another voice, with its prim English accent?

'Harry here, lover,' he growled.

'Harry! I've been trying to reach you all day.' Her tone was petulant. 'Your secretary said you'd gone out of town.'

'That's right. Look, Renee, I have to see you. How about tonight?'

His request was greeted by a stony silence.

'Renee? Are you there?'

'Aren't you going to ask *me* why I wanted to get in contact with *you* first?'

'What?'

'Why is it that men can't think of more than one thing at a time, especially when they've got sex on their minds? Things must be bad for you to want to see me on a week night.'

Her comment rankled. 'You know me so well,' he said drily.

Her laugh was not a nice one. 'Heavens, no, Harry. I don't know you at all. Not the real you. Only that part which occasionally dominates your thought processes. I'm sorry, lover, but no. I have a million and one things I have to do tonight. I'm flying to Melbourne first thing in the morning. A conference. A colleague was supposed to go, but he's sick and I've been designated his substitute. That's why I was trying to ring you, to let you know.'

'Damn.'

'I'll be back by Saturday.'

'That's three bloody days away.'

'You could always come with me,' she suggested coyly. 'My nights are free.'

'But my days aren't. I have things I have to do this week.'

'You wouldn't come,' she threw at him, 'even if you didn't.'

'No, Renee, I wouldn't.'

'Can't blame a girl for trying. So… I'll see you Saturday night. Dinner first?'

'If you insist.'

'I insist. And afterwards…your place or mine?'

'Mine,' he ground out, then actually felt guilty. Because he knew he would not be thinking of Renee that night, but the girl down the hall. He *wanted* to think of Tanya. That was why he'd said his place. Harry always claimed to be honest with his women but this wasn't honest. This was using Renee in the worst possible way.

'Renee?' he added sharply.

'Yes?' she asked hopefully.

'Nothing,' he muttered. The alternative, after all, was even more wicked. He could not— would not—do it. 'I need to know the name of a place I can take a girl to get her a complete makeover. A one-stop salon which does the works. Hair. Nails. Skin. Body. Make-up. Money's no object. I want the best. And I want it for tomorrow.'

Again, there was a chilly silence on the other end of the line.

'Renee?' he prompted.

'I'm here, Harry. Is this a work thing?'

'No, it's private.'

'I see. So who *is* this needy female, might I ask?'

'Just a girl.'

'Is she the reason you went out of town?'

'Yes.'

'And you brought her back with you?'

'Yes.'

'She's *staying* with you? In the penthouse?' She sounded shocked. And well she might. Harry normally never let females stay at the penthouse. One night was their limit.

'Yes,' he ground out.

'How long for?'

'Indefinitely.'

'Why?'

'You don't need to know that, Renee.'

'I think I do.'

'She has nothing to do with you and me.'

'No kidding. Does anything?'

'What do you mean by that?' he snapped.

'I mean, Harry, that unless you tell me who this girl is and what she means to you, we're finished.'

'Is that so?'

'That's so.'

'Looks like we're finished, then.'

She swore at him in a very unladylike fashion then slammed the phone down.

Harry banged the receiver down as well and held it there, breathing deeply in and out. What in hell did you do that for, you idiot? he asked himself angrily. Now you're really up the creek without a paddle, aren't you?

'Damn and blast,' he swore. 'Damn and bloody blast!'

Harry snatched up the receiver again and punched in the number for Wild Ideas. The receptionist would be gone by now, but there was always someone there to answer the phone till at least eight. His staff put in long hours.

'Yes?' a female voice answered impatiently.

'That you, Michele?'

'Yes.'

'Great. You're the one I actually wanted.'

'Boss?'

'The one and only.'

'Where are you? I had a couple of questions I wanted to ask you about the Packard Foods account yesterday, but Sally said you were out of town and couldn't be contacted.'

'I was, but I'm back now. What's the problem?'

'No worries now. Peter straightened me out.'

'Great. I've got a small job for you that's urgent.'

'Harry,' Michele groaned. 'It's nearly six and Tyler's picking me up at seven to take me to some swanky do. I have to go home and make myself gorgeous before then.'

'That's all right. This won't take you too long. You might know it off the cuff. All I need is the name and number of a top beauty salon. The kind that gives women the works. You know the sort of place I mean. You go in looking like a bag lady and come out like a supermodel.'

'Oh, I see,' she said waspishly. 'You think I'm a regular customer of such a place, do you?'

Harry had to laugh. 'Well, hell, honey, you sure glammed yourself up all of a sudden a while back. I hardly recognised you.'

'I did that all by myself, Harry,' she pointed out drily. 'With a little bit of help from Lucille.'

'Who's Lucille?'

'A neighbour and good friend of mine.'

'Do you think she'd know of such a place?'

'Perhaps. Lucille is always perfectly turned out. She has a glam look to go with her glam job.'

'Which is?'

'She's a relocation consultant.'

'A what?'

'She finds people places to live.'

'Single?'

'Divorced.'

'Age?'

'Thirtyish.'

'Can I have her number?'

Michele laughed. 'You're wasting your time, Harry. Lucille is still going through her man-hating phase after a particularly bad marriage. Even if she was on the way to recovery, she can't abide playboys. She's met a few in her time and thinks they're to be avoided at all costs. She took some convincing before she believed Tyler had changed his spots, I can tell you.'

'Men don't change their spots,' Harry said. 'They just con women into thinking they have.'

'You are such a cynic, Harry. Look, I'll find out what you want from Lucille and give you a call back later tonight? What number should I ring you on?'

He gave her his main home line, not his private unlisted number. 'Thanks, Michele.'

'No trouble. Just one question.'

'What?'

'Who's it for?'

'Just a friend.'

'Since when do you have women who are just friends?'

'Now who's the cynic?'

She laughed. 'Have to fly, Harry.'

He hung up as well, half expecting the phone to ring as soon as he did. But it remained silent. Renee, it seemed, had really finished with him.

Strangely, Harry felt nothing now but relief. Next, he called Richard, who sounded more than relieved that everything had gone off so well.

'She sounds different to what I expected, though,' Richard said. 'Smarter.'

'She is,' Harry agreed. 'She *sounds* smart too. Her good old dad didn't do much for her in life, but he at least left her with a great speaking voice. The shareholders are going to be impressed, I can tell you. And the staff at Femme Fatale too, I'll warrant. All I have to do is smarten up her appearance a bit.'

'What's wrong with her appearance? The report said she was attractive.'

'Attractive for a barmaid in the bush does not cut the mustard as the head of Femme Fatale. And her clothes are all wrong, which is one of the reasons I'm ringing you. Where's Maxine's wardrobe?'

'I have it all here, in my garage, in two huge suitcases and various other assorted bags.'

'Could you drop them over to my place some time tomorrow? Just leave them with whoever's on the desk.'

'Will do. When do you think you'll be taking her in to Femme Fatale?'

'First thing Friday morning.'

'Then I'll have to call Bob Barr and tell him you're coming in. I haven't said anything to him so far, but he'll have to be warned, otherwise he'll be seriously cheesed off. He has a huge ego, has Bob.'

'Mmm. I have a few reservations about your Mr Barr. If he's as brilliant as his reputation, why hasn't he done better with Femme Fatale? The company was basically in good shape when Maxine died.'

'He claims Maxine invested far too much into the perfume she wanted to launch. A project he immediately cancelled.'

'Yes, I know. I was going to do the advertising campaign. But why cancel? You can't recoup an investment by opting out, only by going ahead. There's huge profits to be made in perfume. Provided it sells, of course. And Wild Ideas would have seen to that.'

'I'm not sure. I asked him myself the other day and he raved on about cash flow and economic downturns and market fluctuations, and soon my eyes just glazed over. I suggest you talk to him yourself. You have business savvy, Harry. I'm just a solicitor. And a pretty ordinary one at that. You know how hard I had to work to get through law school.'

Harry nodded at the memory of Richard staying up all night studying sometimes. They'd shared a dingy place in one of the seedier areas of Sydney during those long-distant days, Richard's background not being much better than Harry's. Both had been society rejects with nothing going for them but their looks and their wills. Both boys had been determined to make something of their lives, against the odds. And both had succeeded.

Or Richard had till now…

Harry still could not believe his mate's stupidity in borrowing money to buy shares.

'You are sure this idea of yours will succeed, aren't you, Harry?' Richard asked with a return to doubt.

'Dickie boy, you can get that Hermitage out of the cellar and start polishing the bottle right now.'

Richard groaned.

'Have to go, buddy,' Harry said, smiling. 'Or our heiress will wonder what I'm up to.'

Harry found Tanya still chatting away to Arnie, telling him about the view from the balcony. Her eyes sparkled at him as he entered the room and it took all of his control not to go over, take that blasted phone out of her hands and sweep her into his arms.

'Harry's finally back,' she told Arnie breezily. 'I'd better go before he throws me out for spending all his hard-earned money on this call. Yes, yes, I will. Look after yourself now. And don't let Dolly Walton start cooking for you.'

She smiled as she hung up, a strangely knowing little smile.

'What are you smiling at?' he couldn't resist asking.

'Men,' she said.

Harry's eyebrows lifted. *'Men?'*

'Yes. Tell them they shouldn't do something and suddenly that thing becomes the most attractive thing in the world.'

'Er…what exactly are you referring to?'

'Dolly Walton. I've been sneakily trying to get her and Arnie together for ages, but he wouldn't have a bar of her. The moment I warned him against her his tune started changing.'

'Are you saying you *want* Arnie to marry the black widow Walton?'

'Of course. It would be the perfect solution to my worries where he's concerned.'

Harry shook his head in amazement.

But Tanya's words gave him food for thought. She'd begun to grow in attractiveness for him soon after Arnie had warned him off. Was it as simple as that? Did he want her this badly because she'd become forbidden fruit?

It was perverse, but possible.

'Why are you staring at me like that?' she asked, and he suddenly realised he was.

'Sorry,' he muttered.

'It's my hair, isn't it?'

'No. Not at all. I was thinking. Sometimes I stare when I think.'

'What were you thinking?'

'What I can order us for dinner.'

'How about a pizza?'

'A pizza! I thought you liked to eat healthily.'

'Mostly. But I'm human. I happen to like pizza, and the occasional one won't kill me. I don't have high cholesterol, like Arnie. Do you?'

'I have no idea. Never had it measured.'

She looked appalled. 'You really should start looking after yourself, or one day you'll drop dead of a heart attack.'

'Too bad. I have no intention of living any differently or worrying about my health. I work out regularly, which should make up for my small excesses. By the way, I've lined up a place for you to have your hair done tomorrow.'

He decided not to tell her yet she was going to be made over from top to toe. Some things were best sprung on a female. They could be extra sensitive when it came to criticism over their appearance. 'And Richard is bringing over your aunt's clothes for you to go through tomorrow night, because, come Friday, you'll be making your grand entrance into Femme Fatale's head office.'

She paled considerably. 'So soon?'

'No point in delaying.'

'I...I'm going to be horribly nervous, Harry.'

'That's only natural. Just don't let your nerves get the better of you.'

'How do you do that?'

'You focus.'

'Focus?' she repeated, tilting her head charmingly to one side.

'You put your mind firmly on what you want. Then you let nothing—and I mean nothing—get in your way of getting it.'

Harry tried not to take his own words literally, because if he did he'd be lost, and so would she. He wanted her as he'd never wanted a girl in all his life before. But he could see nothing but disaster ahead if he let his hormones rule his head.

'And what is it that I want in this case?' she asked him, oh, so ingenuously.

'The respect of your staff,' he stated firmly, 'and the revitalisation of your company.'

'*My* company…'

'Yours, Tanya. Always remember that. Femme Fatale is yours.'

'Mine,' she repeated, and started gnawing at her bottom lip. When she finally let it go with her teeth, it was all pouty and dark pink.

Harry was beginning to have uncontrollable thoughts and urges again when the phone rang. Renee, he suspected as he picked up the phone, willing to beg his forgiveness. He might even forgive her this once, at least till he had Arnie's little girl safely back home.

'Harry Wilde,' he announced brusquely down the line.

'Harry. It's Michele. Quick, wasn't I? Lucille said the place to take your girl is called Janine's. It's in North Sydney, in an old house in a side-street, handy both to your place and the office. I have the address and the phone number. Do you have a pen?'

'Fire away.' He jotted down the details as she briskly relayed them.

'Lucille said they wouldn't be fully booked on a Thursday. She said to warn you that they're poisonously expensive but worth every cent, although she also said they don't actually turn bag ladies into supermodels. But I assured her that no female you took up with would be a bag lady in the first place. She said to know exactly what you want, especially in the hair department. The hairdressers there have strong opinions of their own and like to talk their clients into them.'

'Don't worry,' he ground out. 'I know exactly what I want. And woe betide them if they don't follow orders.'

CHAPTER ELEVEN

'*SHORT?*' Tanya echoed in horror. 'And *straight*? And *black*? Are you *sure* that's what Harry said he wanted?'

'Your man-friend was most insistent, honey,' the campy hairdresser said. 'And he's so right. You're going to look cool.'

Tanya didn't want to look cool. She wanted to look feminine, and sexy. 'But I want it creamy blonde,' she groaned plaintively. 'And wavy. Down to my shoulders.'

'Sorry, darls, your ends are far too damaged to ever be creamy blonde again. And I daren't risk any more bleach on these poor abused roots. But not to worry. You're going to look fab. Short hair's very in, you know.' He gathered up the straw mass in one hand and twisted it back tightly from her face. 'Look. It suits you short. You have such great bones, not to mention a gorgeous long neck. But here's

Janine. I'll just check again with her before I start, shall I?'

Janine was a hard-faced blonde in her fifties and the owner of the place Harry had driven her to that morning. Tanya had swiftly gathered it was not just a hairdresser's, but a trendy beauty treatment salon. It had depressed Tanya when Harry had ordered the works for her. Wasn't there anything about her he liked?

'Mr Wilde was most insistent,' Janine confirmed. '*Very* short and *very* black were his orders. He said he would be most displeased if we changed anything. Clearly he has a vision of how he wants you to look, my dear,' she added, with a hint of something which made Tanya's skin crawl. 'Of course, if you'd like to call him…'

The last part of Tanya's usual decisiveness died at that point, as had her overnight belief that Harry had begun to find her not only good company but almost attractive. Those long looks he'd given her last night over the pizza dinner hadn't been admiration, she now realised, but his working out what he would change, and how. He'd been planning her makeover, not falling victim to her charms as she'd so stupidly hoped.

She sighed. 'Just do whatever Mr Wilde wanted.'

Which they did—for the next eight hours! Her hair was ruthlessly cut and brutally coloured blue-black, her entire skin surface mercilessly exfoliated and steamed. Everything that could be waxed was waxed. Her body was massaged and moisturised, pampered and pummelled till she could have screamed. Her eyebrows were plucked and shaped, and her nails manicured and painted.

Thankfully, they also fed and watered her at intervals, otherwise she might have passed out from hunger and dehydration. Breakfast that morning had been black coffee and a skinny slice of left-over pizza, Harry promising to have his fridge and cupboards fully stocked that day.

Around four Tanya was allowed to discard the white towelling robe which had been her uniform for most of the day and re-dress in the grey woollen skirt and pale pink twinset she'd donned that morning, after which she was led back into the room where her hair had initially been chopped off and where a stunning-looking girl named Chelsea set to making up her face, explaining as she proceeded exactly what she was using and how to use it.

Clearly Tanya was expected to make herself up fully ever day. Also clearly Harry hadn't been happy with her efforts up till now.

'I'm using a light beige colour,' Chelsea said as she applied the cool liquid. 'It has an SPF30 built in to protect your skin from further damage.'

Tanya had already been chided at length about her sun-damaged skin, another self-esteem-boosting experience. Fortunately she was young, she'd been told. It would quickly recover with the right care and the right products.

Translucent powder followed the foundation, then her eye make-up. The girl carefully applied a dusky blue eyeshadow, black eyeliner, and heaps of black mascara.

'I'm making your face up to complement evening wear,' she was told. 'I gather from Janine that Mr Wilde is taking you out to dinner tonight. During the day I would suggest a more subtle look, with a grey eyeliner, not so much mascara, and very little to no eyeshadow. Your eyes don't really need it.'

Tanya began to listen intently as her face took shape under the girl's expert hand. The last thing applied was blusher, something Tanya had never used, thinking it was something old ladies needed, not younger women. She was amazed at the result, the way it highlighted her cheekbones and gave her face a vibrant glow.

She really did look striking, even with that silly shower cap still on her head. They'd done a very good job on her eyebrows, giving them more of a curve which opened up her eyes and gave her a slightly saucy and challenging expression.

It seemed to say that this was not a woman to be tangled with.

When the hairdresser returned, to remove the moisturising cap and blow-dry her hair, Tanya's amazement kept on growing.

'You see?' he said when he finally finished and picked up a mirror to show her the back. 'Fab, honey. Just fab.'

Tanya could still hardly believe her eyes. The short black hair didn't look at all harsh or mannish on her, not with her face made up that way. The sleek, slicked-back style highlighted the size of her eyes, and, yes, made her neck look impossibly long. She turned her head this way and that, liking her hair from every angle.

'Happy with it?' the hairdresser asked smugly.

'Very.'

'I think your Mr Wilde's going to be happy with the finished product as well,' he said with a knowing wink.

His use of the phrase *finished product* put paid to any raising of any silly hopes in *that* direction. Because that was exactly what she was to Harry. A product.

He wanted her to look the part she was about to play, that of a confident and competent businesswoman. As much as the new hairstyle and hair colour suited her, it was still a very businesslike look, and made her look older. Harry wasn't interested in her person- ally, or physically. To keep letting her mind float in that direction was the way to hurt and unhappiness.

The 'finished product', however, had re- stored some of Tanya's teetering self-esteem. At least she could walk into the Femme Fatale office tomorrow morning feeling confident of her appearance. That was something!

Harry headed for Janine's to pick up Tanya right on five, as organised, having spent a most unproductive day other than organising a gro- cery delivery. Big deal!

He hadn't been able to put his mind to any- thing creative or constructive. And now here he was, parked outside Janine's, waiting for Tanya to appear, feeling apprehensive.

It worried him that it no longer mattered what Tanya looked like. It was the girl herself who entranced him. The person he'd shared a pizza with last night, that delightful creature who'd chatted so naturally whilst stuffing her face, regaling him with stories of the weird tourists who'd stopped at Drybed Creek thinking it was *sooo* romantic. He'd laughed with her over that, privately thinking that the only romantic thing about that particular place was Arnie's little girl.

The truth was she could shave her head bald and cloak her body in rags and he'd still want her. Having her hair cut ruthlessly short was not going to work.

Harry hadn't anticipated, however, that the move to make her less attractive would fully back-fire on him.

The door to Janine's opened and she came sashaying towards the car, looking nothing at all like Arnie's little girl, but a different creature altogether. A sleek, sophisticated, *striking* creature on whom that severe short black hair looked sexy as hell. As she drew closer his flesh tightened at the challenging arch of her redefined eyebrows, the elegantly long curve of her exposed neck, the provocative fullness of her expertly outlined lips.

He glowered with disgust at the perverseness of fate, leaning over to throw open the door for her.

'You don't like the way I look,' she said straight away on climbing in.

'It's not exactly what I envisaged.'

The dismay on her lovely face made him feel dreadful. But he refused to start complimenting her. Already her body language suggested his approval meant far too much to her. Bad enough that he wanted her. If she started wanting him back then things could quickly get out of hand.

'But you'll do, Tanya,' he said curtly. 'You'll do. Now, let's get you home and find you something suitable to wear for tomorrow. Richard should have dropped off your aunt's things by now. And the groceries should have arrived as well. I was going to take you out to dinner tonight, but something has come up and I have to go out.'

And wasn't *that* the truth!

'Oh…' Her disappointment was acute, telling Harry he was doing the right thing in avoiding her tonight.

He suspected he'd be doing a lot of avoiding during the coming month. Tomorrow at Femme Fatale would be okay. They wouldn't be alone, for starters, and his mind would be solidly occupied on the mission at hand.

But the weekend ahead loomed as a problem. He'd have to make some excuse not to show her around Sydney, as he'd promised, then find someone else to do the honours, some sensible female who wouldn't lead her astray. Looking as she looked now, men would be jumping out of the woodwork to get to the revamped Tanya.

Too bad Michele was shortly to be married otherwise he would have asked her. Michele was an eminently sensible female. Maybe that girlfriend of hers, Lucille, could be coerced into playing tourist guide and chaperon. If she was going through a man-hating phase then she'd be perfect!

Harry was still pondering this course of action an hour later whilst he prowled through the penthouse, waiting for Tanya to come out and parade the outfit she'd picked out of her aunt's wardrobe. She'd refused to let him have any say whatsoever in what she wore tomorrow, but had still wanted him to wait and give his approval.

He hadn't wanted to wait for a second. Hadn't wanted to be alone with her just now. He wasn't himself at the moment. He'd used some of the time to shower and change from his business suit into casual grey trousers and a pale blue jumper. Shortly he aimed to take a taxi down to the yacht club, of which he was a member, work himself to a frazzle in their gym, drink himself silly at the bar, then roll home well after Arnie's little girl would have retired for the night.

'Well, what do you think?'

Harry's head snapped up at her voice. He'd been pacing the main living room and smoking like a chimney in a vain attempt to calm down.

The sight of her curvy figure poured into a body-hugging scarlet suit reversed the effects of his last six cigarettes, sending his heartbeat way up till the blood was thrumming in his temples like jungle drums.

He dragged in deeply on the last centimetre of his current cigarette, but his eyes never left her. Hell, he had to get out of here. And *now*!

'The price-tag was still on this,' Tanya said, her face slightly flushed with pleasure over how she looked, and possibly at how he was staring at her. 'It was wickedly expensive.'

And wickedly sexy.

'I didn't like the idea of showing up in my aunt's office in something she'd already worn,' she was saying. 'So this should be perfect, don't you think?'

'Perfect,' he repeated through gritted teeth. Bob Barr's eyes were going to pop out of his head.

'All her clothes fit me like a glove,' she rattled on. 'Even her shoes. These are gorgeous, aren't they?' she said, holding out a foot and turning her ankle this way and that to display the matching shoes.

Harry stared in grim silence at the shapely ankle and stockingless leg.

'She has some gorgeous accessories too. And some really swish costume jewellery. What do you think of these earrings?' She touched the classy gold and garnet drops which swung sexily against her swan-like neck.

Harry's fingers itched with the need to stroke it, to stroke all of her body. He could see it now, not in that scarlet suit, but naked, every womanly dip and curve just aching to be caressed, and kissed, and…

'I really have to be going, Tanya,' he grated out, the coldness in his voice at odds with the heat in his flesh. 'It's gone six-thirty. Sorry to leave you alone, but there's plenty of food, and the television has cable as well, if you're interested.'

All the sparkle drained out of her eyes. 'You're going out with Renee, aren't you?' she accused.

'Yes,' he lied.

The look on her face just killed him.

Her shoulders sagged. She turned and walked slowly away, back towards the room he'd put her in, the one furthest from his. He stared after her, and before he knew it he was hurrying, not towards the front door, as decency demanded, but after her.

He caught her at her door, spinning her round and pulling her into his arms. 'I lied,' he blurted out. 'I'm not going out with Renee. I broke off my relationship with her last night.

I was going out just now to get well away from you.'

'*Me?*' She gaped up at him.

'Yes, *you*, you silly little fool. You've been driving me insane. It was bad enough before you came out dressed like that. I thought I could resist you. But I find I can't. And I'm sick to death of trying.'

'But…but I thought you didn't like the way I looked this afternoon.'

'I *love* the way you look. And I want to make love to you till I drop. It's just that I promised Arnie to look after you, damn it all, and I don't think he had making love to you in mind when he said that!'

Hell, why was he babbling away like some guilt-laden idiot? He'd already made up his mind, hadn't he? He'd already crossed the line. He was a goner and so was she!

But it was Tanya who finally made the next move, winding her arms up around his neck and pressing herself against him.

'Arnie always thinks he knows what's best for me,' she murmured. 'But he doesn't. I happen to think making love to me at this moment would be the perfect way of looking after me.'

Yet still he hesitated, compelled to warn her before taking what she was offering him. 'Always remember it's just sex with me, Tanya. Nothing else. Never think it's anything else with me.'

Something darkened in her eyes, but she didn't flinch or look away. 'I know that, Harry. I'm not a child. Or that much of a silly little fool.'

'Don't tell me you love me. Don't *ever* tell me that you love me.'

'Harry,' she retorted, sounding both exasperated and frustrated, 'please just shut up and kiss me.'

He swore under his breath, then kissed her, and kissed her, and kissed her, still half afraid to move on, afraid over what he was getting himself into here. Till finally kissing her just wasn't enough. He needed to feel *all* of his body covering hers, not just his mouth. He needed more than his tongue inside her.

As the more familiar feelings of lust kicked in, Harry's emotional confusion receded, his very experienced male body taking over where his less experienced heart had been left floundering.

Stripping her was the first essential, his hands on autopilot as they reached for the buttons on her jacket. In no time she was naked to the waist, her bra on the floor, her deliciously full breasts quivering under his touch, her nipples stiffening into his palms.

When she moaned, a red-hot haze of desire spiralled him well out of range of any revival of conscience. The zipper of her skirt fell easy victim to his fingers and pooled at her feet.

'Kick your shoes off,' he ordered thickly, and she did so, her body bare now except for a high-cut scrap of white satin.

He swept her up into his arms and carried her over to her bed, which was unfortunately covered in her aunt's discarded clothes. They didn't stop him. Not for long. His passion made him strong, holding her effortlessly with one arm whilst he swept back the bedspread with the other, all the clothes tumbling with it over the end of the bed.

And then he was drawing her down with him, drawing her down into the cool depths of the clean cream sheets into a world where he'd been so many times before.

But never with anyone like this...

She gasped with what almost felt like surprise when his mouth finally found a nipple. And blushed when he removed her panties. She sucked in sharply when he touched her between her legs, then trembled uncontrollably when he kissed her there, moaning softly. When he abandoned her for a short while to go to his room and return with protection, she didn't move a muscle. He found her still lying as he'd left her, her legs apart, her arms flopped wide, her eyes glazed.

Yet her spreadeagled body didn't look in any way wanton, or lewd. He was touched by the intensity of her arousal, and the evidence of it before his eyes. He fell back upon her without further foreplay, unable to wait any longer before plunging his own aching desire between the lips of her glistening flesh. She cried out, then clung to him, whimpering with pleasure as he rocked rapturously into her.

How hot she was! And tight. Deliciously, exquisitely tight. It would be so easy to forget everything but his own pleasure.

But to do so would be to be like *el creepo.* As selfish as Harry could be in bed, he simply could *not* be with Tanya. She deserved better. She deserved the best.

So he put his mind elsewhere and waited till her nails started to dig into his back and her hips lifted upwards to meet his. Then and only then did he thrust more powerfully, filling her totally with each downward surge. Her nails dug deeper, but he didn't mind. He relished the pain, and the urgent way she was gripping him, both inside and out.

He felt her come, the spasms literally taking her breath away—and his too—propelling him swiftly to a climax which went on and on and on.

God, he thought, his head whirling. God…

His heart was still thudding several minutes later, the storm very slow to subside. At last she went limp in his arms, groaning when he eased himself away and out of the bed for the necessary trip to the bathroom. He regretted having to leave her, even briefly, returning to find she'd pulled a sheet up over her nakedness. The look she gave him was decidedly dazed.

His heart tightened a little as he climbed back under the sheet with her. Guilt again, he presumed. Though it was a little late for that.

'Come here, you gorgeous thing you,' he growled, and drew her back into his arms.

When she settled, with her head on his chest and her left arm encircling his waist, Harry lay back and let out a deep and highly satisfied sigh. For a guilty man he sure felt fantastic, totally relaxed in every pore of his body. He didn't yearn for a cigarette to soothe any lingering agitation this time. All he wanted was to lie there and hold her, savouring the experience.

His mind drifted back over her various responses. He suspected she'd never had a man lick her naked nipples before, let alone anywhere else. He suspected there were a myriad different things she'd never done before.

Harry was grateful *el creepo* had been such a klutz in the cot.

She stirred a little in his arms, lifting her head to glance up at him. 'Is it always like that for women when they're with you?' she asked wondrously.

Harry knew exactly what she was talking about. Females having orgasms during intercourse weren't nearly as common as the women's magazines liked to claim. Neither was the lack of an orgasm always the man's fault, though he could certainly make his partner's coming more likely.

Orgasms began in the brain, not the body. And Tanya's brain had been very turned on from the moment he'd first kissed her. Harry would have liked to take all the credit for all her pleasure, but the truth was she'd been ripe and ready for him.

Again, Harry believed he had *el creepo* to thank for that. He'd primed her up, but left her wanting.

'Not always,' he told her truthfully. 'I think you desperately needed being made love to properly,' he added, and her eyes jerked up to his.

'You think so?'

'Yes, I do. I don't think your Robert did much of a job of introducing you to sex, Tanya.'

Her head lifted higher off his chest. 'You think *Robert* introduced me to sex?'

Harry was taken aback. 'Are you saying he *didn't*? That he wasn't the first?'

'I… I…'

He saw distress in her eyes. And fear.

He didn't want her looking at him with either emotion.

'I'm sorry, sweetheart,' he said swiftly. 'I shouldn't have brought the subject up. How many men you've been to bed with is none of my business. I was a bit surprised, that's all. Believe me, I'm glad that you *do* have a sexual past, otherwise I wouldn't be here with you now. As much as I fancy you like mad, I gave my word to Arnie to bring you back to Drybed Creek the same way you left. He thinks you're a virgin and I thought so too, till you told me about Robert. That's why I jumped to the conclusion he was your first and only lover.'

She continued to stare at him. 'Are you saying you *wouldn't* have made love to me if I were a virgin?'

If Harry was strictly honest, he probably still would have. Eventually. 'I…er.. certainly would have fought a more gallant fight against my baser instincts.'

'*Baser* instincts?' she repeated, her nose wrinkling.

'Basic, then,' he amended. 'We all have *basic* instincts, Tanya. Yours were on the warpath tonight. You wanted me, honey. And you needed me, in the most basic of ways. So don't start denying it now.'

She didn't say a word, but her eyes carried shame and confusion. Harry wasn't keen on the shame. He was beginning to get just a tad annoyed with the situation. And with her. Damn it all, it was just like a woman to decide afterwards she'd done something to be ashamed of when beforehand she'd been all for it. They never could make up their minds!

'We had sex, honey,' he ground out. 'Great sex. And you had an orgasm which nearly took your head off. Face it. You're a highly-sexed creature. You just needed a man with a bit of know-how to bring it out in you. Now, you can either go back into your prissy I've-been-conned-and-hurt shell, or you can keep on being a grown-up woman with grown-up desires. Which is it to be?'

Her chin shot up and her eyes flashed daggers at him. 'Don't try to manipulate me for your own ends, Harry Wilde. I'm awake to you with your reverse psychology ploys. I have never been prissy and I take full responsibility for my own actions tonight. Please feel totally exonerated from any guilt, if that's what's making you so angry. But also please don't make Arnie any more silly promises, because you and I both know that where sex is concerned you're utterly incapable of keeping them. You're as big a liar as Robert, too. Just a more devious one.'

'What?' he thundered.

'You know and I know that you didn't fancy me like mad all along, not till you broke up with your girlfriend and made me over into something closer to what turns you on. I'll bet Renee's a brunette with short hair. But not to worry. I'm not complaining. Look what I got out of it. An orgasm to take my head off, as you so delicately put it. And I'm sure there are more where that one came from.'

Harry was flabbergasted by her attack.

'But not tonight,' she said crisply, before he could tell her that Renee had shoulder-length red hair. 'I've had a big day and there's an even bigger one tomorrow. Femme Fatale, remember? Right now I need a nice long relaxing bath, followed by some food and eight hours' sleep. So if you don't mind...I'd like some privacy...'

An uncontrollable fury was heating Harry's blood. Now he knew why he'd been reluctant to get involved with this...this...harridan. Arnie had warned him she was a difficult person to live with. He'd just received his first lesson! And how! She and Renee were a pigeon pair!

'Fine,' he said testily, and vacated the bed before realising that his anger had somehow transferred into a fierce hard-on. Her blushing at the sight of it reminded him that she wasn't really like Renee.

She talked tough, but she wasn't tough. Not when she was in his arms. She was like melting chocolate.

He smiled a devil's smile at her and thought not of tomorrow morning but tomorrow night, when he would show her that she might not *always* be responsible for her actions. Sex was a very powerful force, and sexual satisfaction a compelling and corrupting need.

He would make her a slave to that need. He would make her crave it. He would make her beg.

'Your wish is my command,' he drawled. 'Just call me if you want your back scrubbed.'

And he left her to it.

CHAPTER TWELVE

Tanya waited till she heard a door bang in the distance, then jumped out of bed and raced over to close and lock the bedroom door. Then she raced back and threw off the sheet she'd been hiding under, her eyes widening when she saw the dark red stains on the cream sheet.

'Oh, no,' she groaned. She'd been worried she might have bled. But not that much. The pain had only been minimal, passing as quickly as it had come. She'd cried out more in shock than in agony.

That Harry hadn't noticed her virginity at the time didn't really surprise her. He hadn't been expecting it, for starters. And she hadn't exactly acted like one. Lying there with her legs wide open and letting him do whatever he liked with her.

But, ooh…the pleasure of his mouth on her down there.

But nothing had compared with what had followed. Harry had been right about that. Her head *had* nearly come off.

Harry had said it wasn't always like that with the women he'd been to bed with, but she suspected it was most of the time. He was an incredible lover. Tender, yet masterful. Imaginative and passionate. Exactly what she'd thought he would be.

But an incorrigible playboy, as Arnie had warned her. All he wanted from her was what Renee had once given him. Sex, without strings. Sex, without commitment or consequences.

Don't ever tell me that you love me, he'd warned.

Tanya had no intention of doing so.

And she had no intention of ever letting him know she'd been a virgin before tonight.

Ripping off the bottom sheet and the mattress protector, she carried them into the bathroom where she set about washing away the evidence of her innocence. Clearly Harry liked his women experienced. Well, she was experienced now, wasn't she?

Harry said to get what you wanted you had to focus. Tanya aimed to focus. On being the sort of woman Harry wanted. And then she would get what *she* wanted.

Harry.

'How do you think I look? Is this suit really all right for today?'

Harry did his best to give her a cool once-over, but Tanya in that red suit did not inspire cool, any more than she had the previous evening, floating through the penthouse after her bath, dressed in white satin pyjamas, humming whilst she cooked herself a huge omelette, then squatting cross-legged on the sofa in front of the television whilst she ate it. By the time she'd gone to bed Harry had had to plunge himself into the longest coldest shower of his life, after which he hadn't thought his privates would ever see the light of day again, let alone with an erection.

Clearly, he'd been wrong.

'Don't you think the neckline is a little low?' he said testily.

'Do you think so?' Her hand fluttered up to cover the hint of cleavage, her eyes suddenly not sure.

He liked it that she seemed a little nervous this morning, and more like the Tanya he'd first brought to Sydney. The bold display she'd put on after her bath the previous evening had irritated the death out of him. Because she wasn't fooling him one bit. Even if she'd bonked every second bloke in Broken Hill, she was still a babe in the woods when it came to men. Before last night she'd probably only ever experienced the wham-bam-thank-you-ma'am kind of sex. Come tonight, he aimed to start introducing her to the finer points of erotic experience. He didn't want her pretending she'd already been there, done that, because he knew she hadn't.

The thought stirred him. Far too much.

The last thing he wanted was to walk around in agony beside her all day. Even that *hint* of cleavage had to go!

'Yes, I do,' he said firmly. 'You're trying to impress today on a business level, not seduce every man you meet. So go and put something on underneath that jacket. And take off those earrings, for pity's sake.'

She did so, looking momentarily crushed. He hated seeing her like that but it was all for the best. He would let her wear them tonight, when she was totally naked. He would tell her how beautiful she was like that, and how sexy, and how much he wanted her.

'There…there's a cream satin camisole which might do?' she suggested hesitantly.

'Anything,' he bit out, though hessian was preferable to satin. Satin gave rise to images of those darned pyjamas again.

The cream cami hid the cleavage but didn't entirely dampen his ardour. Harry shook his head. Poor Richard. Maybe his fortune and his future were lost after all. Nothing worse than putting either into the hands of a lust-crazed fool. Which was exactly what Harry was at the moment. A most unusual occurrence. He hadn't been this fired-up over a female in years.

Actually, he'd *never* been this fired-up over a female, a thought which momentarily flummoxed him.

'Come on,' he ground out. 'Get your bag and let's get going. It's gone eight.'

Harry sighed a weary sigh and headed for the front door, a bleak-faced Tanya in tow.

Tanya sat silently beside Harry in his sleek black car, hating herself for her loss of confidence this morning, both in her appearance and her ability to hold Harry's sexual interest. He seemed so irritated with her all of a sudden. Impatient and uncomplimentary. If he thought the red suit unsuitable, then why hadn't he said so yesterday? Why wait till this morning, when he must have known she'd be extra nervous?

Maybe he'd decided overnight that he didn't want to go on with their sexual relationship but just didn't know how to say so. Men always went quiet when things were bothering them.

Harry remained exceptionally quiet during their drive to Femme Fatale's factory and head office, which he'd curtly informed her over breakfast was in Surrey Hills, an old inner city suburb which was on the other side of the city centre.

She tried to enjoy the drive over the Harbour Bridge and through the city streets, but her inner misery made her blank to her surroundings. They were stopped at a set of lights in heavy traffic, tall buildings stretching up on either side of her, when it all finally got the better of her.

'If you want to leave things at a one-night stand,' she snapped, 'then just say so. Don't give me the cold shoulder.'

To give him credit, he looked truly taken aback. He also looked so handsome and sexy this morning it was incredible to think she'd been in his arms the night before, drowning in those beautiful grey eyes, being kissed by that lovely sensual mouth. She still hadn't run her fingers through his hair, but she'd like to. She'd like to do a lot of things with him, and to him.

The thought that their affair was already over sent her heart plummeting.

'What makes you think I would want to leave it at that?' he asked, his eyes searching hers.

She shrugged. 'Just a feeling.'

'Then you couldn't be more wrong,' he muttered. 'Do *you* want to leave it at that?'

'Heavens, no!' she gasped.

Harry tried not to smile. But what other woman would be so open and ingenuous about her wishes? He loved it that there was no overt manipulation in her. No artifice. She wanted him. He could see it in her eyes.

He leant over right then and there and kissed her full on the mouth. 'Being with you is heaven,' he murmured against her lips. 'What man gives up ambrosia after one small taste?'

The horns honking behind forced him to drive on, but his lips tingled with the sweetness to be found in her mouth. He could not wait for the day to be over. He could not wait for this night to come.

Tanya sat there, glowing. He still wanted her. He'd called her heaven to be with. She was in heaven herself, basking in his compliments, and his desire.

She felt so happy that she stopped being nervous about the day ahead. Nothing mattered as much as having Harry still want her. Nothing.

Ten minutes later, Tanya was stepping out of Harry's Porsche into a small concrete car park beside a warehouse-type building which boasted the Femme Fatale name in bold red lettering on all the grey outer walls.

Some butterflies reappeared when Harry took her elbow and led her round onto the street and in through the front door into a modern reception area, decorated in grey and white, with striking red plastic chairs lined up against the walls. The pert and pretty blonde sitting behind the grey desk looked up as they entered, enquiring brightly if she could help them.

'We're here to see Mr Barr,' Harry told her. 'Could you let him know that Mr Wilde and Ms Wilkinson have arrived?'

Tanya was startled to hear Robert's surname.

'Did…did you say Mr Barr?' she whispered to Harry while the girl rang through to announce their arrival.

'Yes, that's right. Bob Barr. He's the business consultant Richard's firm put in charge.'

Tanya felt faint. 'Oh, dear God,' she choked out.

Harry looked alarmed. 'What is it? What's wrong?'

'It's Robert.'

'Robert who?'

'*My* Robert,' she whispered.

'*Your* Robert?'

'I think so,' she replied weakly.

Harry looked disbelieving. 'Sydney has over four million people, Tanya. Names are repeated everywhere. It couldn't possibly be the same man.'

'It is if he's in his mid-thirties, with black hair, blue eyes and a dimple in his chin, wearing a suit which might not live up to the one you're wearing today but would run a close second.'

A white door leading out of the reception area opened and a smoothly suited male of around the right age walked in. His wavy black hair, piercing blue eyes and movie star dimple rather confirmed his identity to a shocked Harry.

El creepo in the flesh.

Unfortunately, he didn't live up to Harry's preconceived image of a man who'd be pathetic in the cot. He looked as if he'd know his way around a woman's body on automatic pilot, as well as every trick in the book. And then some.

Harry wanted to pulverise the suave bastard for seducing his girl, and spoiling his illusions about the extent of her innocence.

'Mr Wilde,' old blue eyes said smoothly, holding out his elegantly manicured hand.

Harry shook it with a steely grip. Hell, the creep was a good-looking rogue. The sort women fell for like a ton of bricks.

'Richard rang to tell me you were coming and bringing Ms Wilkinson with you,' he was saying. 'We haven't met, but I've heard all about your success with Wild Ideas, of course. I gather you did the advertising for Femme Fatale in the past. And, speaking of Femme Fatale, I'm delighted to hear that our mystery heiress has been found at last. How do you do,

Ms Wilkinson?' he introduced himself to Tanya with formal politeness, shaking her hand.

Harry's eyebrows arched cynically once he realised Barr didn't recognise her face, let alone her name.

Of course not, he sneered silently.

She hadn't been a person to him. Just a lay.

Someone to amuse himself with for a while.

Had he laughed over her lack of experience behind her back? Had he enjoyed making her fall in love with him, then taking all she had to offer in the name of love?

What that might have entailed wrenched at his very soul.

'Welcome to Sydney,' the creep was saying to her while he continued to hold her hand. 'And to your inheritance. I've been doing my best to get Femme Fatale back into shape after the tragic death of your aunt, but things haven't been easy, what with the resignations of key staff and a most unfortunate business decision your aunt made to venture into perfume. That cost the company a bundle. But you don't have to worry your pretty head about such things.' He smiled an oily smile down at her. 'You can leave the worrying up to me.'

Harry glared at Tanya. Why wasn't she saying something? Why wasn't she tearing her hand away and telling the smarmy bastard to rack off? Why was she staring up at him with almost frightened eyes? Didn't she know he couldn't do anything to her now, not unless she wanted him to?

Was that it? She still loved him and wanted him?

Harry felt quite sick at the thought.

'You don't recognise her, do you?' he broke in brusquely, and Barr blinked surprise at him.

'I beg your pardon?'

'Don't beg *my* pardon,' Harry ground out. 'Beg Tanya's.'

'Tanya's?' Now something twigged in his sleazebag mind and he stared hard at her.

'My God,' he rasped. 'It's Tanya. From the motel at Broken Hill.'

Tanya at last found her voice.

'Yes, Robert,' she said. 'It is.'

'But you...you look so different. Your hair. Your face. Your clothes...'

'Amazing what you can do with a little money,' she returned with superb cool.

Harry was so proud of her. And heartily relieved. This was not the voice of a girl still in love.

'Shall we go into your office, Robert?' she added with even more cool. 'There's something we have to discuss.'

Barr looked worried. And well he might, Harry thought with malicious glee.

Barr led them back through the white door he'd opened earlier and into a large room divided into glass-topped cubicles. He didn't bother to speak to any of the women seated behind their desks, despite their looking up with curiosity. He marched down the central corridor and on through a door, beyond which lay a small office where a thin, tired-looking brunette of around forty was seated behind a desk. She looked up expectantly, first at Tanya and then at Harry, who remembered her as Maxine's secretary, though her name eluded him.

'Hold all calls, Leanne,' Barr told her on his way past, rudely making no introductions.

The woman's expression was a classic behind *el creepo's* back. No love lost there, Harry noted wryly. Obviously Barr's good looks were no compensation for his arrogantly high-handed manner. It was no wonder the company wasn't doing well if he treated all the staff like that.

Maxine's once plain but functional office had been renovated, Harry also noted, with flashier teak furniture and a new deep blue carpet with gold diamonds on it. The gilt-framed painting on the wall behind him looked anything but a cheap print. The carved drinks cabinet in the corner was well stocked as well, with crystal decanters and a silver ice bucket. Harry wondered how Barr could justify such expense when he was only there on a temporary consultancy basis.

Unless, of course, he'd been planning a longer stay. Had he thought he'd be able to seduce whatever heiress Richard's firm had found, regardless of age and marital status?

Harry rather suspected he had.

He watched the creep fuss over Tanya, displaying no shame whatsoever, smiling unctuously as he pulled up a chair for her before hurrying round to sit down behind the large, important-looking desk which he no doubt thought reflected his personality.

Harry pulled up his own chair, shooting Tanya a questioning glance, but she wasn't looking his way.

'This is such a surprise,' Barr began. 'No, surprise is not the word for it. Shock would be better. You will have to forgive me, Tanya, if I'm momentarily at a loss for words. The change in you is just so remarkable.'

'Indeed,' she remarked coldly. 'Unfortunately, I don't see any change in you. I think you can safely say your days at Femme Fatale are numbered, Robert. In fact, they're over, as of now.'

Bravo, Harry thought. He could see she was upset, but she was still in control. Beautifully so.

'You can't do that,' Barr retorted, his face darkening.

'Can I do that, Harry?' Tanya asked him with a cool arch of her newly shaped eyebrows.

'You certainly can. You have the power of hire and fire.'

'Then your services are no longer required, Mr Barr.'

'You miserable, vengeful bitch!'

Harry was on his feet in an instant. 'I'd watch your mouth, mate, if I were you. Otherwise you might not get the lovely bonus I was going to pay you to pick up your brief-case right now and get the hell out of here.'

That stopped him in his tracks. The promise of money usually did with creeps. Not that Harry had been talking about money.

'How much of a bonus?'

'Heaps. Come outside with me and I'll give it to you straight away.'

He didn't waste any time. Just swept a few things into a snazzy black crocodile-skin brief-case and stormed out. Harry was hot on his heels, with the memory of a pale-faced Tanya in his mind.

He directed the creep round to the relative privacy of the car park, which was thankfully deserted at that moment.

'Well?' Barr practically sneered. 'Where is it?'

'Here,' Harry said, and jabbed him hard in the gut, twice, with both fists clenched hard. Bam. Bam.

Barr went down onto his knees between the cars, gasping, then groaning.

'And don't even *think* of taking me to court,' Harry threw at him. 'There aren't any witnesses and I hit you where it hurts but doesn't show. Felt damned good too.'

'But why?' Barr choked out once he could breathe. 'What did I ever do to you?'

'It's not what you did to me. It's what you did to Tanya. I know all about you, you lying, two-timing sleazebag. But this time you screwed the wrong woman.'

Barr struggled back up onto his feet, still clutching his stomach. 'But I didn't,' he choked out. 'I swear to you. She's lying if she said I did.'

'Don't give me that bull.'

'It's not bull. Sure, I wanted to. But, hell, she wanted it too. Gave me the come-on with those sexy eyes of hers for days. But when I put the hard word on her she just wouldn't, not till I told her I loved her and said I wanted to marry her. When I finally got her alone in my room, the damned fire alarm went off and that was that. I swear to you, Wilde. *Nothing happened.* Then, when my wife rang the next morning, Tanya wouldn't have anything more to do with me. I think she was more upset that I didn't really love her than the fact I was married.

'Stupid bloody virgins,' he scorned, and Harry froze. 'Hypocrites, all of them. They have to pretend it's love before they can take that final step. I don't usually bother with girls like her, but, hell, she had a certain something which got me in.' He looked more closely at Harry and laughed. 'She's got you in too, hasn't she? That's why you lost it just now. She's got you panting after her like a randy schoolboy. I recognise the signs. I was the same. Just don't forget to tell her you love her, because, believe me, you're not going to get to first base without it.'

Harry was battling not to ram the creep's teeth down his throat while his head whirled at Barr's words.

She *couldn't* have been a virgin. He would have known. He would have *felt* something.

You did, you idiot. Remember how tight she was? And what about that cry when you first penetrated her? And those whimpering moans.

It killed Harry to think they might have been sounds of pain, and not pleasure.

Why hadn't she told him? Why hide something like that? And why had she let him get a lot further than first base *without* the promise of love, or marriage?

Why?

He recoiled from the idea she might fancy herself in love with him. Didn't she know he wasn't capable of loving her back? That the most he could offer her was friendship, and some fun in bed?

Spinning round, he marched back towards the office—and Tanya—determined to get some straight answers. If there was one thing Harry couldn't bear, it was emotional turmoil.

He needed to know where he stood. And he needed to make his own position clear.

Love was not on his agenda. Never had been. Never would be. If she couldn't handle that, then he would have to find another place for her to live for the next month. Because no way could he stand her living under his roof unless she was under him in bed as well. Of that he was equally sure!

'Speaking from man to man,' Barr shouted after him across the car park, 'I'd steer clear of that little missy if I were you.'

CHAPTER THIRTEEN

WHEN she heard Harry come into the outer office, Tanya's heart stopped. When she heard him speak to Leanne, asking her to go get them all coffee and sandwiches, she suspected he was just getting rid of the woman for a while. When he opened the inner office door and glared over at her, Tanya knew he knew.

Her stomach tightened into the fiercest knot.

'Right,' Harry growled, closing the door firmly behind him whilst his eyes never left her. 'This fiasco has gone on long enough. Bob Barr told me his version of the truth, but I want to hear what happened between the two of you from your own lips. And don't even *think* about trying to deceive me like I suspect you did last night, because I have my head into gear now and I'm watching you closely. Liars always give themselves away, provided you know what to look for, and I do, honey. Believe me, I do. I rely on my knowledge of body language a lot in my business. I need to know who's trying to con me and who isn't.'

Tanya jumped up from her chair. 'I have *never* tried to con you,' she choked out, distressed that he would think she'd deliberately set out to deceive him.

'You were a virgin and you let me think otherwise,' he accused. 'You not only implied you'd had a raging affair with Barr, but you said he wasn't your first.'

'No,' she refuted, just as hotly. 'I said Robert hadn't introduced me to sex. And he hadn't. You merely assumed there'd been others.'

'That's playing with words,' he snapped.

'Something you've never done, I suppose?' she countered angrily.

'I don't lie to the women I sleep with. I was straight with you. I warned you beforehand.'

'About what?'

'About the sort of man I am. That it was just sex with me. That I can't stand pretending it's love.'

Tanya tried not to let his words hurt her, but they still did. 'How gallant of you. Then you'll be relieved to know it was just sex with me too.' Not a total lie, since she'd believed it at the time. 'That's why I let you think I'd been around. Because I knew you wouldn't do it otherwise.'

'I don't believe you. Barr said you wouldn't sleep with any man you weren't in love with.'

Tanya was totally taken aback. She hadn't realised Robert knew her that well. Because of course she *had* fallen in love with Harry. She wasn't sure when. The intensity of her desire for him had masked her growing emotional involvement. She hadn't known the truth till this morning, when Robert had walked back into her life and her only concern had been the fear of losing Harry. It wasn't the sex she feared losing either, but the man himself. His respect. His admiration. His friendship.

So what to do now? How to handle this for the best?

Don't ever tell me that you love me, he'd said.

So what *was* it that Harry wanted from his women? Not love, that was for sure. Or any kind of clinging or mothering. Tanya suspected he liked them independent and strong and spirited. He wouldn't want her backing down to him, or crawling, or begging.

'Is that what's worrying you?' she mocked. 'You think I might be in love with you?'

'*Are* you?' he demanded to know.

Tanya hoped her face wouldn't betray her.

'Don't be ridiculous!' she scoffed, using exasperation as a blind. 'What's to love? You're too self-centred and arrogant to love. But I do want you, Harry Wilde. I have since the first moment I saw you.'

His nostrils flared slightly at this confession, his eyebrows lifting with a type of shock. Tanya decided he didn't look too displeased, however.

'I might have still been a virgin when I met you,' she went on, 'but my so-called affair with Robert had opened my eyes to a side of myself I hadn't known existed. I'd never been turned on before, you see. Not even remotely. Maybe because I hadn't met the right type of man. Robert turned me on, not just with his looks but his manner. He was so smooth and so self-assured. He said all the right things, made all the right moves.'

'Good old Bob.'

Tanya heard the sarcasm in Harry's voice and thought, *Goodness, he's jealous! He must care about me a little to feel jealous.*

It was a confidence-boosting thought.

'But not even Robert prepared me for the feelings you evoke in me, Harry. A fire alarm wouldn't have stopped me if it had been *your* motel room I was in that night. So I wasn't going to let a little barrier like virginity come between us last night. You yourself told me what to do when I wanted something. You told me to focus, and not let anything get in my way. Well, I focused last night and I got what I wanted. Was that such a crime? All right, I lied by omission. But you should still have guessed I'd never done it before, Harry. Why didn't you?'

'I don't make a habit of deflowering virgins,' he bit out. 'You're my first, to my knowledge.'

'No kidding? Well, it didn't hurt you, did it?' she taunted softly.

'Don't, for pity's sake,' he groaned, raking his fingers agitatedly through his hair. 'I know now I must have hurt *you* last night. Yet I was totally unaware. I can't begin to tell you how that makes me feel.'

'How does it make you feel?' she asked, surprised by his expression of guilt.

'Like a bloody animal,' he snarled. 'Which I'm not.'

'Of course you're not,' she choked out, and went to him, cupping his face gently before finger-combing his dishevelled hair back into place. 'I thought you were wonderful,' she whispered as she wallowed in touching him. 'And just what I wanted...' Harry Wilde, out of control, wanting her with a passion that didn't stop to question, or think.

'Stop doing that,' he snapped, grabbing both her wrists. His eyes glittered a steely reproach at her. 'Keep that up and you'll have what you want again,' he ground out. 'Right here. And right now. And to hell with the fact that Leanne will be back shortly with the coffee and sandwiches. I'm sure we have enough time for a quickie. We don't even have to undress.

I'll just bend you over the desk there and hitch your skirt up. You'd be surprised how easily an enamoured man can find his way through pantyhose without removing them. I could be inside you in less than ten seconds. Does that thought turn you on?'

She stared up at him, not sure that it didn't.

His mouth twisted when she didn't say a word.

'Make up your mind, honey,' he drawled, letting her wrists go and lifting one hand to her mouth while the other trailed seductively down her throat. Teasing fingers brushed over her startled lips. Others found a breast through her clothes, kneading it, teasing it, making the nipple ache and burn within her bra.

Everything was beginning to spin out of control in her head, and in her body. Only the thought of the secretary returning stopped Tanya from surrendering to whatever he wanted. She could not bear for anyone else to see her like this. Love had made her shameless. But not *that* shameless.

'No,' she moaned, and wrenched her mouth away from his hand. 'Not here.'

His other hand immediately dropped away from her body. 'Good decision. Office quickies don't really do much for me any more. I like my sex slow and prolonged these days. So do most women, I've found. Till tonight, then.'

It was a statement, not a question.

Leanne's knock on the door was a relief.

'Hold it there,' Harry called out to the secretary. 'And I'll open the door for you.'

Tanya watched Harry go and open the door, amazed at the speed of his transition from ruthless seducer to cool businessman. She hated to think of him doing what he'd just done to her with a zillion other women. But she could not deny the excitement he generated within her. Or the need. It was intense, that need. A physical craving which was wriggling and worming its way all through her. She really didn't know how she was going to get through the day.

Harry couldn't bear the way she was looking at him, with such overt sexual hunger. Didn't she know you didn't look at men like that these days? Certainly not a man like himself. Not unless she wanted him to take outrageous advantage of her all the time. As he'd just done. Almost.

But, damn it all, it *was* what she wanted from him, wasn't it? Sex. Nothing else, really. Not love or caring or commitment. Just sex.

Now why didn't that thought sit well on him? It should have. She was the supreme male fantasy: a beautiful and willing young woman, inexperienced but eager to learn, an avid student of the erotic arts with him the master. What more could he possibly want? Why wasn't he thanking the stars for the sexual *carte blanche* she'd given him, instead of feeling so damned disgruntled?

Male ego, Harry decided ruefully. He'd wanted her to be in love with him, wanted her to have been compelled last night, not by desire but by a depth of feeling far surpassing anything she'd felt for Barr.

Instead she'd labelled it as 'just sex.'

Hah! It hadn't been *just* sex. It had been *great* sex. *Fantastic* sex. *Spectacular* sex. They'd clicked in a very special way. That was why he couldn't wait for more.

Yet he'd have to. She'd said no and Harry was a man who respected that. Besides, there was a job to be done here today. Harry wasn't about to forget that. Though he had a few minutes ago, hadn't he? He'd been letting her get to him, as Barr had said.

He really had to get his head out of his trousers.

'Leanne,' he said abruptly, and the secretary's head jerked up from where she'd been setting out the coffee and sandwiches on the desk. 'I want you to tell us what's been going on here since Maxine's death. Tell us exactly what Bob Barr's been doing wrong.'

Leanne frowned. 'Mr Barr left, has he?'

'Your new boss fired him,' Harry said, nodding towards Tanya.

Leanne beamed at Tanya. 'That's fantastic! Everyone's going to be thrilled to bits. That man's caused nothing but trouble since he arrived. Riding roughshod over everyone's feelings. He has no idea how this place works.'

'And how *does* it work?' Tanya suddenly piped up, sitting down in Bob's vacated chair and looking as if she'd been made for it.

Harry could hardly believe she was the same nondescript girl who'd been behind the bar of that outback pub, barely…what? Three days ago?

The change in her *was* incredible. He had to agree with Barr on that count. So much more confidence, and style. A woman, not a girl. A formidable woman with a mind of her own. A butterfly emerging from its cocoon, getting ready to spread her wings and fly.

And fly she would one day. Away from him.

Harry was shocked at how despairing that thought made him feel.

It took him a few seconds to accept the un- acceptable, to believe the unbelievable.

Harry Wilde, falling in love for the first time in his life…

Harry felt a moment's fury at fate. This was not what he wanted!

But that attitude didn't last long. He'd al- ways been a pragmatist and a realist. No point in denying something just because he didn't want it to be so.

How ironic, he thought as he watched Tanya trying out her new wings, that the one woman who'd managed to capture his elusive heart only wanted what he'd once thought was all he was capable of giving. Sex.

Harry had to smile. Life was cruel. No doubt about that.

Still, he would enjoy giving her what she wanted, in a bittersweet way. And who knew? Maybe if he played his cards right…

But, hell, how did he do that? He'd never wanted a woman to fall in love with him before.

It would be a challenge all right.

Harry's spirits perked up considerably. He did like a stiff challenge. The trouble was he had absolutely no clues how to go about this one. He would have to play it by ear…

Tanya was screamingly aware of Harry's eyes on her as she spoke to Leanne. They weren't lewd in expression. Or even seductive. It was more a thoughtful gaze, a steady, rather speculative regard.

If she hadn't had an involving distraction she might have been totally unnerved.

Fortunately, she was soon fascinated by what she learnt about Femme Fatale and Robert's appalling mismanagement. There was nothing really wrong with the company—or not according to Leanne—although the resignation of key staff had hurt them. The three woman had left as a result of 'personality clashes' with Mr Barr. First had gone the national sales manager, then their chief overseas buyer, then one of their best product managers.

'Personality clashes?' Tanya queried, seeking further explanation.

Leanne shrugged. 'Mr Barr didn't take kindly to personal rejection. Neither did he ever appreciate that Maxine often hired women executives like herself.

'And I don't mean lesbians,' she added, when she saw the startled look on Tanya's face. 'I'm talking about strong, independent, creative, self-motivated women with minds and opinions of their own, who naturally resented Bob Barr's overbearing and patronising style of management.'

'Barr was a damned fool in more ways than one,' Harry pronounced, with a warm, meaningful glance Tanya's way.

Tanya glowed under his compliment. With a confidence that would later astound her, she called for the heads of the various departments to be brought in to meet with her, to discuss what had been happening under Mr Barr's misguided direction and to be assured that things would be different from now on. She would be seeking their help and advice, as she was new to the lingerie business.

She heard similar stories of Robert's stupidity from Sales and Marketing, Personnel, Accounts, the mail-order section and, finally, the new product development division. The very assertive brunette in charge of that department was still furious over Robert's cancelling the perfume project she'd worked on with Maxine.

'That bastard didn't have a creative bone in his body. And not a scrap of integrity. He called me a dyke, then cancelled my pet project, simply because I refused to go out with him. I like men, as it so happens. I'm married to one. *You* don't hit on married women too, do you?' she aggressively asked Harry.

'Not me, ma'am,' a startled Harry defended whilst Tanya tried not to laugh. But the woman really was a bit scary in her anger.

'That's good. We've had all the womanisers round here we can take!'

'I'm just Ms Wilkinson's minder,' Harry declared. 'Won't even be here in future. Just today.'

'Good. You're too damned handsome to be hanging around a factory full of women. They'd never get any work done with you around all the time.'

'Tell me all about the perfume project,' Tanya interrupted firmly, not wanting to start thinking about Harry's being handsome and sexy and irresistible. Which he was, damn him!

When the woman was finally gone, Tanya leant back in the desk chair and looked over at Harry. 'You meant that?' she asked.

'Meant what?'

'About not coming in with me any more?'

'Yes, I did. Look, Tanya, I've seen the way you've operated here this morning. You're a natural leader and organiser. On top of that, the women here like you, whereas I'd just rub salt in the wounds Barr made. Of course you'll need help. But you can jot down any questions or queries you have during the day, and we can discuss them over dinner each night.'

'But…but…'

'But nothing. You were born for this, honey. You know it and I know it. Just focus and you'll be fine. So will Femme Fatale. To show you how confident I am, I'm going to ring my broker this very day and buy some more shares. Can't have Richard being the only one making a fortune out of this.'

'What about me? Aren't I supposed to be making a fortune out of this as well?'

'Honey, we both know you're not going to sell those shares of yours. You're hooked.'

'I…I'd certainly like to give running Femme Fatale more than a month's trial. I mean…there's no reason for me to leave after that annual meeting, is there? If the shares have risen by then, your friend can sell his and get his money back. You can even sell yours and make another fortune. But I'd like to stay on, regardless.'

'Then do it. Stay on.'

Tanya was fired up by Harry's confidence in her, but she knew it wouldn't be as easy as all that. Still…nothing ventured, nothing gained. 'I'll have to find somewhere else to live,' she said.

'Why? You're welcome to stay with me for as long as you like.'

Tanya was shocked, then quite overcome. 'You…you mean that? I won't be in your way?'

'Honey, *honestly.*' His smile was wickedly sexy, his eyes so hot on her it was indecent. 'How could you possibly be in my way? I'm crazy about you. You know that. I was even going to suggest you move into my bedroom for the duration, to save me traipsing down that long hallway to your room every night!'

Tanya swallowed at the thought of sleeping in his bed every night, of being able to roll over and touch him whenever she felt like it, of his doing the same to her.

'Well?' he prompted. 'Would you like to do that?'

'I... I...yes, I guess so,' she agreed, blushing fiercely. Damn it all, when was she going to stop *doing* that?

He smiled. 'Great. Because, let's face it, you're going to be putting in long hours here during the week, so we'll only have the evenings to be together. And the weekends, of course. But I have plans for them. We can't spend every weekend in bed together,' he said, and Tanya wanted to tell him she wouldn't really mind.

'Firstly, I want to show you all of Sydney. Then I have this hankering to dress you up in something incredibly sexy and glamorous and take you to the opera one night. Do you like opera? A new season is about to start at the Opera House.'

'I don't really know,' she said, still feeling slightly shell-shocked by this development. 'I've never been.'

'Then it's high time you did.'

Tanya loved his plans, but felt a measure of panic that she would fall so deeply in love with him that she would never crawl out of the black pit after their affair was finally over.

And it would be over one day. Harry was not a marrying man. He was a playboy. And playboys didn't fall in love and settle down with one girl for the rest of their lives. Harry claimed to be crazy about her, but that was because she was new to him. New and different. Tanya suspected that now he was over the shock of her being a virgin he was looking forward to impressing her with his sexual know-how.

Tanya had to concede she was too. But along with the excitement and anticipation lay apprehension.

'What happens when you get bored with me in bed?'

Harry shrugged his broad shoulders. 'I could say the same of you, Tanya. Maybe one morning you'll wake up and not want me to make love to you ever again.'

She stared at him. He wasn't talking about her. He was talking about himself. Because that was what always happened to him. One day he woke up and found that the woman snuggled up next to him left him cold.

'I doubt that, Harry,' she said, refusing to accept his cynical truth as her own. 'I'll always be sexually attracted to you. I can't see that ever fading.'

'How flattering of you to say so. But then…all new lovers think that. Let's just take each day as it comes,' he suggested pragmatically, 'and live it to the full. For who can really guess the future? Okay?'

'Okay,' she agreed. It would probably be the only way she could survive this. To live each day as it came.

'Great. Now, I must go make some important phone calls.'

'Can't you make them from here?' she asked, panic-stricken suddenly at the thought of his leaving her.

'Actually, no, I don't think I can. Too many of them. I'll go to my own office. You'll be fine, Tanya. Just keep focusing. I'll be back to pick you up here at…er…when? Six? Six-thirty?' He stood up and walked over to the office door.

Tanya scooped in a deep breath, letting it out slowly. Harry was right. She couldn't lean. She had to do this all by herself. At least the company would still be there when Harry no longer was. Life went on, didn't it, even if your heart was broken?

'Better make it seven,' she said firmly.

'That's my girl,' he said, grinning. 'But don't work too hard, mind. I want to *take* you to bed tonight, not tuck you in.' And, yanking open the door, he left.

CHAPTER FOURTEEN

'YOU *are* tired, aren't you?'

Tanya lifted heavy eyes from the slice of delicious dessert cake which the waiter had just placed in front of her. 'I think it's the wine,' she said. She hadn't had red wine before and it was having a different effect on her from white, making her more mellow than merry.

Harry smiled a rueful smile. 'I'll take you home.'

'But you can't! I mean…we haven't eaten our desserts yet, and I know they must have cost a small fortune. I saw some of the prices on the menu.' They were in a lovely but very expensive restaurant overlooking the Harbour, with beautiful white linen tablecloths and a marvellous view.

'To hell with the money. I'm taking you home to bed.' And he raked back his chair and stood up.

'Oh.' If she'd been feeling sleepy a second ago, she suddenly woke up at the word *bed*.

Five minutes later they were on their way, with their untouched desserts in a carton resting on Tanya's lap.

'It was nice of the waiter to let us take our desserts home, wasn't it?' she said, in an attempt to make conversation. Nerves were gathering in the pit of her stomach. Had Harry meant bed, bed, or that other kind of bed, where sleep wasn't first on the agenda? She hoped he meant the latter. She didn't think she'd be able to sleep tonight without completing what Harry had started earlier that day. She'd successfully ignored her stirred up body all afternoon, but now, it was back with a vengeance, her heartbeat quickening, the blood roaring around her veins. When she rolled down the window of the car, letting in the cooler night air, goosebumps prickled all over her rapidly warming skin.

'Nice, my foot,' Harry snorted. 'I'd paid for them.'

'It was still nice of them,' she repeated stubbornly, and Harry smiled over at her. God, he was gorgeous when he smiled. He was gorgeous when he *didn't* smile. He was gorgeous all the time.

'You're right,' he agreed, if a bit reluctantly. 'They could have refused. They don't exactly specialise in takeaway.'

'I'll enjoy eating mine much better later,' Tanya said. 'That was a very big meal.'

'We'll eat them in bed together,' Harry said. 'Afterwards.'

'Oh,' Tanya gasped, her cheeks flushing at the decadent image of them sitting up in bed, totally naked, devouring the rich chocolate cake.

'You're not *too* tired, are you?' he queried, sounding a little worried.

'No. But I...I could do with a bath first.' Now that he'd confirmed what he meant by bed, Tanya was hotly aware of the fact it had been a long day, with many hours since her morning shower.

'How about we have one together?' Harry suggested.

Tanya's stomach turned over at that idea.

'I don't know if I'd like that or not,' she told him truthfully. 'I might go all shy on you.'

'Why would you go all shy, a girl with a great body like yours?'

Tanya was startled that he thought her body was so great. It was adequate, in her opinion, but nothing out of the ordinary. She had nice enough boobs, she supposed. But her shape was very hourglass, not the sleek, athletic look which seemed popular these days. She never exercised, and she wasn't into sport, so her curves were soft. She didn't have a super-flat rock-hard stomach, or toned biceps, or toned anything for that matter. All she had was what God had given her, which was a tall frame which could thankfully support her C-cup breasts and child-bearing hips without her looking in any way dumpy. Her legs were the only part of her she ever worked out, and that was only because when she walked she walked fast, a habit from her childhood when she'd run a lot to keep up with her long-legged father.

'If the idea bothers you,' Harry went on, his handsome face suddenly serious, 'then don't do it. I don't want you to ever do anything with me you don't want to do, Tanya. Not ever,' he stressed.

'Thank you, Harry,' she said, touched by his unselfish consideration. 'I appreciate that. But I'd *like* to have a bath with you. I really would. I'm just being silly. Recently deflowered virgins do have their limitations and drawbacks, I'm afraid. You'll have to be patient with me.'

He slanted her a slightly sardonic look. 'Patience is not something I'm famous for.'

Tanya laughed. 'What happened to your *I don't want you to ever do anything you don't want to do* offer?'

'That still stands. It's up to me to persuade you over to my point of view.'

'So how do you aim to persuade me to have a bath with you tonight?'

'Would the offer of a million dollars do?'

'Goodness. Having baths with women must be one of your all-time favourite pastimes if you're willing to go that far!'

'Would you believe me if I said I'd never had a bath with a woman before?'

'No.'

'Well, yes, you're right. I have. But not for a damned long time. I certainly haven't since I moved into the penthouse. I don't make a habit of asking women to stay either, not for more than a few hours. So you can count yourself lucky. You're the first female I've ever asked to live with me, do you know that?'

'You...you're asking me to *live* with you?'

Harry slanted her a sharply frowning look 'What did you think I meant when I said I wanted you to move into my bedroom? What else would you call it?'

'I...I don't know. I guess I thought it was just a convenience for both of us, on a kind of till-it-didn't-suit-either-of-us basis.'

He scowled, but didn't deny her interpretation of his offer.

'Living with someone involves a bit more commitment, wouldn't you say?' Tanya went on, determined to let Harry know she knew the score here. She wasn't about to play the fool for another man. Robert had been one too many! 'There's an unspoken promise that the arrangement might lead to something else.'

He frowned.

'Let's face it, Harry, any relationship with you is not leading anywhere else. You have bed-partners, not partners. Which is fine by me—honest,' she hastened to add, lest he think she was putting any pressure on him. 'I mean, I adore you, Harry. You're a fantastic guy. You're great company and a great lover. Just what I need at this point in my life. But I'd rather not think of what I'm doing as living with you. It's more of an affair. A…a fling. An…experience.'

'An *experience*?' he repeated, glowering over at her.

'A *wonderful* experience,' she assured him. 'And one I'll never forget. But let's face it, Harry, one day you'll want to move on. And so will I.' She'd have to, once he tired of her. Which he would.

His brutally honest words echoed through her head once more. *Don't ever tell me that you love me…Always remember it's just sex with me… Never think it's anything else with me…*

He stared over at her, his eyes angry for a moment. Then he laughed.

'This is going to be one *hell* of a challenge.'

'What do you mean?'

'I mean, honey, that I'm going into un-charted territory with you here.'

'I'm not sure what you're getting at. Are you talking about my having been a virgin?'

'Not exactly. But that might be a part of it. Yeah, I think perhaps it might be a *large* part.'

'You're talking in riddles, Harry.'

'Life is full of riddles, my darling girl. None more bewildering than what goes on between men and women. So, do I have to get down on my knees and beg, or will you do what I want tonight out of the spirit of it being an…experience, one I promise you you won't forget?'

Tanya had to laugh. 'You know darned well I don't stand a chance of saying no to you. All you have to do is start kissing me and I'll be putty in your hands.'

'Is that so? Thank you for telling me that. Such knowledge is power.'

'As if you didn't know already!'

'A man sometimes needs reminding. But I won't forget again. Trust me.'

Trust him?

Tanya didn't trust him an inch. But that didn't stop her loving him with all her heart, and wanting him with a want which was reckless in the extreme.

Their arrival in the car park beneath Harry's building brought an end to any smart repartee and a return to tension for Tanya. She clutched the carton containing the desserts during her ride up to the penthouse, almost grateful for its protection, because Harry was suddenly looking at her as if *she* was dessert, and he was about to gobble her up without a by-your-leave.

'Best put them in the fridge,' he suggested gruffly as soon as they were inside. She hurried to do so, thinking it might give her a moment to gather her wits, but Harry followed her into the kitchen, and the second her hands were empty he drew her quite forcefully into his arms.

'Now we'll see how the land lies,' he growled, his mouth bending.

Robert had been a good kisser, smooth and practised, but Harry was something else. He didn't kiss so much as seduce with his mouth, slow and sensual and wet, till she was desperate for more. More of his tongue, more of everything. Her body was leaning into his, pressing and urgent, when he suddenly stopped.

Her eyes lifted to his, wide and hungry.

'Excellent,' he said, with dark triumph in his voice and his face. 'You have five minutes.'

'To do what?' she asked breathlessly.

'Whatever you like while I run our bath and get things ready. Change into something more comfortable, if you like.'

'But I thought we were going to have a bath together.'

'We are.'

'Then what's the point of my putting anything else on?'

His eyebrows arched. 'You don't want to slink around in something sexy first?'

'I don't have anything really sexy to slink around in.'

He laughed. 'Honey, those white satin pyjamas you wore last night are so sexy it's a crime to wear them in front of a guy, especially with *your* nipples.'

'Oh. I...I didn't realise.'

'You could always try on your birthday suit.'

'Walk around naked! Oh, no, no, no, I couldn't do that.'

He looked at her, the corner of his mouth lifting in the smallest of smiles, and she knew she *would* be walking around in front of him naked before he was finished with her.

The idea made her head spin and her heart race. 'You're a wicked man, do you know that?'

'You shouldn't have told me the secret to your co-operation.' And he swept her back into his arms, kissing her this time till she would have stripped off then and there if he'd asked her.

But he eventually put her aside, turned her round and gave her a tap on the backside. 'Now, go be a good girl and make yourself scarce for a few minutes. I'll come find you when everything's ready.'

Delays were never good, in Tanya's opinion. It gave you time to think, to cool down, to worry. Nerves sent her racing to the toilet, after which she stripped off her clothes, cleaned her teeth, then dragged on the white satin pyjamas. She thought of redoing her make-up but decided that was a bit foolish. At the last minute she retrieved her bag from the kitchen and fished out the matte scarlet lipstick she'd worn that day. She was repainting her lips with it in the dressing-table mirror in her room when she spied Harry in her doorway. She didn't turn round, just stared at his reflection in the mirror.

The business suit he'd been wearing that day was gone, replaced by a dark green silk robe, sashed loosely around his hips. He looked very naked underneath. And very aroused.

'Don't stop,' he said thickly. 'I like that red lipstick on you. And put those earrings back on that you were wearing this morning. The gold and garnet ones. I like them too.'

She blinked. 'Earrings? With pyjamas?'

'You won't be wearing the pyjamas for long.'

Tanya swallowed. He wanted her wearing earrings while she was naked. Dear God…

She did what he wanted.

Of course.

She did everything he wanted that night.

Of course.

And it was all mind-blowing.

Of course.

A long time later—it must have been close to dawn—she lay with her head on his chest and her arms wrapped around him, listening to the slow, steady beat of his sleeping heart.

He was exhausted, the poor darling. And so was she. Little wonder. They'd made love so many times and in so many ways she'd lost count.

They hadn't been able to get enough of each other. It hadn't just been Harry. She'd been insatiable, once she'd moved beyond the slight worry he might find her inhibited and boring. What she lacked in experience she'd certainly made up for in her willingness to please him. It hadn't just been desire which had inspired her hands and her lips, but love. She had exulted in the thought she was making love to the man she loved, not just lying there and letting him use her body for sex. It had been a deeply emotional journey for her, and one she would remember till her dying days.

Which, of course, was why she couldn't sleep. Her mind and her heart were too full. How hard it had been not to speak honestly of her feelings when he'd been making love to her so tenderly that last time. She could almost have believed he cared about her when he'd oh, so softly licked her over-sensitised nipples, when he'd slipped gently into her, in the face to face position, for once, then looked deeply into her eyes while he'd pumped slowly into her, going on and on till he'd come one last incredible time.

She'd come too. Amazingly. She hadn't realised a woman could come so many times in one night.

But she had. When it had happened, he'd closed his eyes on a raw groan.

He'd staggered from the bed afterwards, warning her when he returned that that was it. He'd had it. If she wasn't satisfied now, then she would have to wait till morning.

She'd smiled and told him he didn't have to worry about the morning. They had the whole weekend, didn't they?

He'd groaned again, but was soon asleep. Which was fine by her. She could tell him she loved him while he was asleep. She could touch him and kiss him and pretend this was for ever. Because it was. For her. She was a for ever kind of girl.

A tear slipped out and rolled down her cheek.

'Oh, Harry,' she said, and pressed her lips to his skin. 'I do so love you. If only you loved me back.'

CHAPTER FIFTEEN

'IT'S just as well it's a warm night, or I'd freeze to death. Well, don't just stand there with your back to me, Harry Wilde. Turn round and tell me how I look.'

Harry was out on the terrace, smoking. He took one last drag and threw the cigarette over the railing. He knew what he was about to see. He'd seen it earlier that day in the boutique, where he'd bought Tanya two incredible outfits. One for the gala première at the opera tonight, and one for Michele's wedding the following weekend.

He'd been a fool to dress her in clothes of his choosing. But then, he *was* a fool...over her.

He turned, and tried not to stare.

What had looked wonderful on her in the dressing room now looked simply breathtaking. Strapless and white, the gown was beaded over her breasts, with a long sleek shiny skirt which slid seductively over her thighs as she walked.

She came towards him, tall and elegant, a matching stole around her bare shoulders, white satin gloves right up to her elbows. What looked like diamonds sparkled at her throat in the early evening light and at her ears and around her wrist. She was clutching a white satin evening purse.

Harry looked into her large violet velvety eyes and felt his love for her kick him hard in the stomach. His gaze dropped to her mouth, but the sight of those darkly lush lips didn't help. Her image tonight was one of a very sexy woman of the world, far older than her twenty-three years. She'd become a true *femme fatale* during the past few weeks, a woman men would go to war for.

This last thought momentarily distracted him.

'What's wrong?' Tanya queried. 'Don't you like this dress on me any more? Is it the jewellery? You think it's too much? They're not real diamonds, you know. They came with Auntie's clothes. Same with the gloves and bag. Look, if you don't like something, *say* so! Don't just stand there, frowning.'

'No, no,' he returned swiftly. 'You look lovely. I just had an idea, that's all, for your new perfumes.'

'Oh? What?'

'What say you name each successive scent after a famous *femme fatale* in history? Women like Helen of Troy, Cleopatra, Salome, Mata Hari and the like. The ideas for ads would be limitless, and very original.'

'Oh, Harry!' she exclaimed. 'That's brilliant. Why, you clever, clever man! I'd kiss you if it wouldn't do dreadful things to my lipstick.'

'Don't worry,' he said drily. 'I'd prefer it if you didn't. The last time you kissed me I ended up under your desk.'

Did she blush? He doubted it. But who could tell under that skilfully applied mask of make-up?

It had been nearly a month since he'd brought her to Sydney. One marvellous yet miserable month during which he'd done everything he could think of to make her fall in love with him. He'd made love to her till he dropped. He'd taken her everywhere she wanted to go. He'd talked to her for hours over dinner every night about her ideas for Femme Fatale, and watched while she grew into the remarkable woman she'd always promised to be.

The AGM was this coming Monday, but it was really a *fait accompli*. She'd already turned around her aunt's company, revitalised and even improved it. She'd enticed back the three women who'd left, re-implemented the perfume project, and contracted Wild Ideas again to do the advertising. She'd streamlined, then expanded their range of lingerie, stopping production on a couple of lines which hadn't made a profit and introducing several that would flatter the fuller figure.

Harry had applauded this idea, knowing how much of the market was lost by just catering to the waifs. Most women were size fourteen, and they wanted to look as sexy as the next woman.

The shares had already charged back up to seventy-eight cents, partly because of Harry's buying a great swag, but mostly from good word of mouth within the company. Harry had no doubt that, after Monday, the price would top the dollar once more. Richard was ecstatic, and Harry...Harry was now the despairing one.

She hadn't fallen in love with him. He knew this for a fact. Tanya in love would betray herself. She'd start wanting him to stop smoking. And maybe even drinking. She'd certainly want to cook for him.

But she never said a word about his smoking. And she hadn't cooked him a darned thing in all these weeks. Not even toast. Not once. Nothing!

All she wanted from him was his business expertise. And his body. Oh, yes, she wanted that all right. She'd turned into a damned sex maniac. For a girl who'd shrunk at walking around naked for him the first night they'd spent together, she'd come a *long* way. It killed him to think he'd taught her everything she knew, only to have some other man—or other *men*—come along afterwards and get the benefit of her expertise in the bedroom.

Though she didn't confine things to the bedroom any more, did she? He wasn't safe anywhere. Worse, he was powerless to resist her. She only had to look at him a certain way and he was a goner. It kept him on a knife-edge of arousal all the time. He didn't dare meet her in her office for lunch any more. Only yesterday Leanne had almost caught them. Tanya had found it funny, but then she'd already been satisfied once at the time.

The incident had highlighted the fact that he was no longer a person to her but a male body, a toy boy to be used to satisfy her increasingly erotic demands. He didn't know what he was going to do when she grew bored with his technique and wanted a different experience.

Maybe it was time he began to protect himself by distancing himself a little. Maybe he had to accept defeat for the first time in his life.

The thought grated on him like chalk on a blackboard.

Whirling away, he snatched up the bottle of chilled champagne he'd left there earlier. Another of his pathetically thoughtful efforts to win the heart of the woman of his dreams. Grumbling to himself, he filled the frosted flute glasses, then turned to hand her one. She placed the satin purse on the railing and took it.

'Is this to celebrate something special?' she asked, smiling one of those sweet smiles of hers which always got to him. Occasionally she forgot to be this year's candidate for Businesswoman of the Year, or the lay of the century, and reverted to the girl he'd first met and fell in love with. Her eyes would soften on him as well, and for a split second he would be tempted to tell her how he felt.

But along with a natural aversion to failure and rejection lay a fear of exposing himself emotionally. What was the point in humiliating himself for nothing?

'The success of the AGM?' he suggested.

'But that's not till Monday.'

'Your success with Femme Fatale so far, then?'

'I owe everything to you, Harry.'

'Nonsense. You've worked very hard. All I did was give advice from the sidelines.'

'You did more than that,' she said, and for a moment he thought she was going to cry.

But she didn't, raising her glass and smiling at him with only a faint shimmering in her eyes. 'To Harry Wilde,' she toasted. 'My mentor. And my best friend.'

They clicked glasses and drank, Harry watching her with wry eyes over the rim of his glass.

He suddenly saw this night for what it was. Her graduation night. She was about to progress from naïve student to fully fledged success story, in every facet in her life. His role in her life would soon be *passé*.

Harry, old man, he warned himself. Get ready for the big kiss-off. It won't be tonight, but soon. Oh, yes…it's going to be soon.

'We've been good together, haven't we?' he said, smiling to cover his pain. God, how did people fall in love more than once? This was murder.

'More than good,' she agreed, but made no attempt to change his tense from past to present.

'Looking forward to the opera tonight?' he remarked casually as he sipped.

'Very much so.'

'I've hired a stretch limo to pick us up.' All done before he'd realised he was wasting his time.

'Goodness,' she said, sipping her champagne. 'I'd chastise you for your extravagance if I thought it would do any good.'

'I like spending money on my women,' he remarked casually, and turned away to refill his glass before he could see if the barb had hit home. Because what would he do if it hadn't? How could he bear it if she didn't care?

Tanya gripped her glass tightly with her gloved hand and tried not to look devastated. Not that Harry would notice if she did. He wasn't even looking at her.

Had he said what he'd said just now quite deliberately? Was he letting her know that his decking her out in designer clothes wasn't a sign of her being anything special to him, that he often gave his lovers expensive gifts as a reward for services rendered?

She sensed a change in him tonight. Every word was laced with something, a hidden poison of some kind. His eyes had been almost angry a moment ago.

Tanya searched her head for a reason. Had she done something to displease him today? Or yesterday?

She didn't think so.

Maybe she was imagining it.

'When do we have to leave?' she asked, and he turned back to face her, his glass filled to the brim.

He drank deeply while he glanced at his watch, a beautiful gold Rolex which had probably cost a small fortune. As had his black dinner suit.

Harry had never looked more handsome, or more out of her league than he did tonight. No matter how good she looked herself, or how much she tried to live up to the sort of woman Harry might want permanently by his side, Tanya never felt confident that their relationship would last. This fear always increased when they were about to go out in public, to places where Harry would meet other women far more beautiful and sophisticated than she could ever be. Invariably she would try to seduce him at moments like this, because sexual success with him allayed her fears for a while.

She'd become rather addicted to seeing him turned on in dangerous places, to reducing him to a total loss of control. She liked it when he was sweating with need and not always able to fully satisfy that need because of where they were. She liked sidling up to him in lifts which weren't empty, touching him under the table in a restaurant, or even when he was driving. A couple of times he'd reefed the car over to the side of the road and called her bluff, oblivious of who might be watching them. Fortunately, those times had been at night, and the tinted windows had prevented their making a public spectacle of themselves. She wondered if she dared start something in the back of the limousine.

'The car is picking us up at six-thirty,' he told her. 'The opera doesn't start till seven-thirty, but there are drinks in the reception hall beforehand.'

Tanya recklessly determined to have his mind on nothing but her by the time they arrived.

But when she placed a provocative hand on his thigh during the drive to the opera, Harry lifted it off and coolly returned it to her own lap.

'Darling heart,' he drawled. 'You really must learn that men like to make the advances. You'll get what you want before the night is out, never fear.'

Tanya's humiliation was acute, and from that moment the evening was an unqualified disaster, in her eyes. She didn't enjoy mingling with the rich and famous in the lavish reception hall, and watching the plethora of glamorous women who gave Harry the eye. One was especially stunning, a blonde with a model-like figure sheathed in a shimmering gold gown. Harry must have spent a good fifteen minutes talking to her.

Tanya didn't enjoy the opera, either. How could she when she was sitting there in a foment of jealousy? She certainly didn't enjoy the drive home, during which Harry seemed a million miles away, or later that evening, when he made love to her with virtually no foreplay, insisting on a position she'd once found incredibly exciting and sexy but which suddenly felt lewd and ugly.

She didn't come. Not once.

Afterwards, he withdrew from her body without a single word and went to have a long shower, leaving her to slump face down in the pillows, weeping.

The following day—Sunday—was even worse, especially when Harry went out without her for lunch, using a meeting with Richard as an excuse. He didn't come home till very late that night, by which time she was pretending to be asleep. He didn't wake her, and once again she lay there for hours, her heart breaking.

She only made it through the AGM the next day because she was so well prepared. But Harry's absence was marked. He had business of his own to attend to, he said.

He did show up for dinner that night, though it wasn't an intimate little meal for two. She and Leanne had organised a party-type affair for the Femme Fatale executives in a hotel. A reward for all their hard work and support. Tanya did her best to join in the celebrations— their share price had passed the dollar mark that afternoon, following her general address to the shareholders—but she was bitterly aware of Harry's offhand mood, and her own flood of tension.

That tension finally burst its banks during the drive home from the restaurant.

'Harry, what is *wrong* with you?' she snapped. 'Aren't you happy things went well for me today?'

His sidewards glance was cold. 'Don't try to pick a fight with me, Tanya. And don't talk rubbish. Why wouldn't I be happy you've turned Femme Fatale's fortunes around? I've made a mint.'

'That's not what I'm talking about. And I'm *not* trying to pick a fight with you. It's just that you've been so moody these past few days.'

'I've had things on my mind.'

'Then *talk* to me, Harry. *Tell* me what's going on. Something is and I…I simply can't go on like this.'

'Can't go on like what? Are you implying I'm cheating on you?'

She stared over at him. '*Are* you?'

'Isn't that just like a woman?' he sneered. 'Just because you're getting bored with me.'

'I'm *not* getting bored with you!'

'Honey, you're the one who didn't come on Saturday night, not me. And you've been coming like clockwork in that position for weeks. It's you who's different, not me. Why don't you admit it?'

'You're the one who's not being honest here,' she choked out. 'You don't want me living you with you any more and you haven't got the guts to come out and say it! You're trying to twist it around and blame me. I *saw* you the other night. You couldn't take your eyes off that blonde. Maybe you haven't cheated on me yet, but you want to. Oh, yes, you want to so much it's eating you up!'

An excruciating silence descended on the car, which lasted till Harry slid the Porsche into its private parking bay and cut the engine.

'Let's not have a scene, Tanya,' he said tautly. 'I can't stand scenes.'

'Well, I can't stand *this*,' she cried.

'What do you mean by *this*?'

'Not knowing where I stand with you any more. How can I happily make love with a man who wishes I was someone else?'

'I think it's *you* who wants *me* to be some-one else,' he said coldly.

'I just want you to be the man I first met. I liked him and wanted him. But you're not that same man. You've changed, Harry.'

'*I've* changed? Now that's funny. That re-ally is. So what do you want to do about it?'

Tanya stiffened. So he was putting the ball in her court, was he? Her heart sank, but pride kept her chin up. 'I'll move back to the guest room for tonight. Then, tomorrow, I'll start looking for somewhere else to live.'

Tanya waited for him to argue, to beg her not to go, but all he said was, 'Fine.'

Tanya went to get out of the car, but Harry stayed put, behind the wheel.

'Are…aren't you coming up?'

'Not right now. There's something I have to pick up at Richard's place.'

Tanya almost laughed. He was lying. No doubt he'd be ringing the blonde from his mo-bile before she was in the lift, and then making a bee-line for her place. He'd know the way. He'd already spent all Sunday there. Richard was just an excuse, a pathetic, patronising excuse!

Tanya came as close to hating Harry as she ever could at that moment.

'Fine,' she echoed bitterly, and slammed the door. She didn't bother to look back, but heard the car roar out of the car park before she reached the lift.

Tears erupted once she was safely inside the penthouse, and she was still crying over an hour later. In the end, she couldn't stand herself any longer, and climbed off the bed, dragged herself into the shower. Afterwards, she wrapped her nakedness in the blue towelling guest robe which always hung on the bathroom door, bypassing all the sexy nightwear she'd collected over the past month—mostly Femme Fatale samples she'd brought home and teased Harry with by trying them on and asking for his male opinion.

He'd liked her in black best of all. Black satin and lace. Pink, too. And purple. Oh, to hell with it. He'd liked her in anything!

Tanya sighed at the memory. He'd wanted her back then. Frankly, he'd wanted her till this last weekend. And then suddenly he hadn't. She didn't really think it was meeting that blonde which had done it. She'd merely been there when he'd been feeling restless.

Maybe Harry's desire for a woman had a use-by date, she speculated. Maybe, after he'd had a woman every which-way he could, his hormones simply clicked off and he was compelled to move on.

Tanya thought about ringing Arnie and crying on his shoulder, but decided not to. She'd rung him every few days since her arrival in Sydney and they'd chatted away about things in general. She'd told him of her decision to stay on for longer than a month, but she hadn't told him about her affair with Harry. For one thing she hadn't wanted to worry Arnie, or to say anything which would spoil his friendship with Harry. They really got along, those two. Harry always took the phone after Tanya had finished and he'd be still going half an hour later.

Man-talk, of course. Mostly sport. Football and cricket. Tennis. Harry did ask some leading questions occasionally about Dolly Walton, but Arnie was playing that relationship close to his chest. Tanya suspected, however, that things were on the move. She often heard Dolly's voice in the background when she called. And Arnie sounded happy, another reason why Tanya didn't want to burden him with her troubles.

In the end, Tanya drank two glasses of Harry's very expensive Scotch and retired in a decidedly tipsy state, plunging into a restless and dream-filled sleep from which she emerged suddenly with a jolt. She fumbled on the bedside lamp and discovered it was just after one. She'd been asleep for less than two hours.

Damn and blast!

The sound of music filtered through the walls of the bedroom and she sat up. It had to be coming from within the apartment, which meant Harry had to be home. But what was he doing playing music at this hour?

It had a deep throbbing beat, which was why she could hear it. The walls of the penthouse were pretty soundproof.

Curiosity had her getting up and pulling on the blue robe before she ventured gingerly out into the hallway, where she stopped and listened. The music was much louder now, and seemed to be coming from the main living area. A female singer was giving voice to a torrid rock number with an energetic drumbeat. Harry liked loud rhythmic music, but he rarely played it in the middle of the night.

Tanya tiptoed down the hallway and in through the open doorway, only to stop and stare at the sight before her eyes.

Harry was sprawled on the sofa facing the picture windows, a cigarette lolling out of his mouth, a half-empty glass of red wine in one hand, his other stretched across the back of the sofa. His suit jacket was carelessly thrown down on the floor, as was his tie. His shirt was undone and he was humming along with the singer. Every few seconds he stopped long enough to gulp down a large swallow of wine.

The bottle, she noticed, was standing on a side table. She couldn't see how much was left in it, but suspected not much, by the look of Harry. He had the air of a man who was well on the way to being seriously drunk.

'Five thousand dollars a glass,' he muttered, totally unaware of her presence. 'Bloody expensive way to get blotto. But what the hell? Have another glass, Harry.' He said, sweeping up the bottle. 'That'll bring the total up to twenty-five grand.'

Tanya's gasp of shock sent his head whipping round. His hands jerked with it, and the stream of wine largely missed the glass, spilling over the glass-topped table, then dripping onto the plush green carpet.

Harry's four-letter word told it all.

But then he laughed. 'Don't tell Richard I spilt some. He's already having a hernia about my drinking this drop.'

Tanya frowned. 'You really went to Richard's tonight?'

'That's where I said I was going, wasn't it?'

'Yes, but…'

'But you thought I was out screwing blondie.' He laughed again, then swigged back what little of the wine had made the glass. 'Sorry to disappoint you. I'm here making a total fool of myself and polishing off a bottle of rare vintage wine which you yourself made it possible for me to enjoy.'

'Me?'

'Yep, you. Richard agreed to give me his prized Grange Hermitage if I could get his money back. He got it back today in full. So I collected my prize. It's worth a conservative twenty-five thousand at auction.'

'And you *drank* it? You're mad!'

'Madness is in the eye of the beholder,' he quipped.

'And you're drunk!'

'Quite. Which is just as well. Because I'm about to say something that I vowed I would never say. But Richard said I was fool not to. Just let me light up first.'

Tanya shook her head while he lit a fresh cigarette and drew back deeply. 'Now, where was I? Oh, yes, making a fool of myself.'

'Can I turn the music down?' she asked, straining to hear what he was saying.

'If you must.'

She walked over and switched off the CD, then moved further into the room, standing rather nervously in front of him, clutching the lapels of the robe together. 'You can say what you have to say now.'

'Thank you for your permission,' he returned drily. 'I trust what I say to you will remain in confidence. I wouldn't want it getting around town that Harry Wilde had lost it.'

'Good grief, Harry, just say it!'

'Very well. I love you.'

Tanya blinked.

'I said I love you,' he repeated impatiently.

'I *heard* you.'

'Well?'

'Well?'

'Well, nothing, I guess,' he muttered, puffing away. 'I just wanted you to know.'

Tanya's head was still whirling. It was only just sinking in. Harry loved her.

'If you love me,' she choked out, 'why did you try to drive me away?'

'Isn't it obvious? Because I know you don't love me back.'

'How do you know that?'

'Because of the things you didn't do.'

'The things I didn't do? But, Harry, I did *everything* you wanted me to do.'

'I'm not talking about sex, damn it! You think that was all I wanted from you? Hell, sex isn't the be-all and end-all, you know. I could have done with a little less sex and a lot more caring.'

'Caring?' she repeated blankly. 'What kind of caring?'

'Good God, if you don't know then I'm not going to tell you.' He sucked in sharply, pursed his lips, then blew out, the smoke shooting right up into her face.

Tanya didn't stop to think. She just marched right on over and plucked the offending item out of his mouth, stabbing it to death in a nearby ashtray. 'I've had just about enough of you smoking these filthy damned things, Harry

Wilde. And I've had about enough of this self-pitying nonsense. You yourself told me not to tell you that I loved you, so I didn't. But I *did* try to show you how I felt in other ways. Robert was right about one thing. I would not have gone to bed with you in the first place unless I'd fallen in love with you. I certainly wouldn't have done any of the other things I've done with you since, either. I *do* love you, Harry Wilde. I love you so much I've been in despair since last Saturday night.'

He looked thunderstruck. 'You love me?'

Tanya sat down beside him on the sofa. 'That was what I said, wasn't it?'

'You're not bored with me? You don't want to leave me?'

Tanya doubted that anyone had ever seen Harry Wilde looking so insecure, or so in need of reassurance. Her heart melting with love, she leant over, cupped his face and pressed her lips to his. 'Never,' she murmured against them.

He grabbed her by the shoulders and kissed her properly. Tanya smiled inside. The old Harry was back again.

'Tell me again that you love me,' he demanded, after some very long, masterful kisses. He tasted of smoke and expensive red wine, a not unpleasant combination.

'I love you,' she repeated. 'Now, tell *me* again that you love me.'

'I already told you twice.'

'I want to hear it again.'

'Oh, all right. I love you. I love you. I love you. Will that do for a while? Now kiss me again.'

'No. Tell me first when you realised you love me?'

'Good God, must I?'

'Yes, you must.'

His sigh was resigned. 'Very well. The first day I took you into Femme Fatale.'

Tanya sat up straight. 'That long ago! Why didn't you say something?'

'How could I when you said it was just sex between us? I...er...told Arnie.'

'*Arnie* knew you were in love with me way back then?'

'I felt I had to tell him. Considering. I didn't want him thinking I was a creep. Because if you think he didn't guess we were sleeping with each other, honey, then think again.'

'But he never said a word to me.'

Harry looked scandalised by such a notion. 'Of course not. We're mates, Arnie and me. Mates don't dob on each other.'

'And what else does your good mate Arnie know that I don't know?' Tanya asked with a mock steely eye.

'Nothing else. But he did give me a little tip to telling when you fell in love with me.'

'Oh, yes?'

'He said you'd start trying to stop me smoking.'

Tanya's heart turned over. 'Which is why you thought I didn't love you,' she murmured. 'Oh, Harry, you've no idea how many times I wanted to say something, but I was afraid to. I know how much you like smoking.'

'Not as much as I like you loving me,' he said warmly, stroking her cheek. 'I'll stop the smoking if you really want me to.'

'You mean that?'

'I do. But be warned, you'll never stop me having a drink.'

'I wouldn't want to. It was the wine which loosened your tongue and made me the happiest girl in the world.'

'How can you be so happy, loving a selfish, arrogant playboy like me?'

'To be honest, I like you a bit arrogant, and you're no more selfish than most men. But your playboy days are numbered. I have plans for you, Harry Wilde.'

'What plans?'

'Didn't Arnie tell you?'

'Tell me what?'

'That I'm a marrying kind of girl?'

'Actually, he did mention something like that. How long do I have before I have to pop the question?'

'A couple of years, I guess. I'm only twenty-three. But I aim to have kids by the time I'm thirty, and I aim to be married to their father.'

'No need to stress about it just yet, then, is there? We can have fun together for a while longer, and leave the big decisions till a later date. What say we toddle down the hallway right now and have some fun?'

'What say we don't?' she retorted, and he blinked.

Tanya stood up and unsashed her robe. 'I always wanted to make love on this sofa,' she purred, and, smiling seductively, dropped the robe at her feet.

CHAPTER SIXTEEN

'I NOW pronounce you man and wife,' the celebrant concluded. 'You may kiss the bride.'

Harry sat there, amazed how touched he'd been by Michele's simple garden ceremony, and by the look which passed between her and her new husband now that they were officially married. When the groom lifted his bride's veil and kissed her, oh, so tenderly, Harry's eyes actually grew moist. Incredible!

In the past, he'd avoided weddings. The cynic in him had found the rosy optimism and over-sentimentality of such occasions cloying in the extreme. What fools, he'd used to think. Almost half of them would be divorced within no time.

Today, however, optimism was strong in his heart. Over half of those marriages would still be solid and strong, he reminded himself. It was really a matter of choice and commitment;

being prepared to work through the tough times, and really appreciate the good; focusing.

Of course it would always help to have an understanding woman as your wife. One with compassion as well as passion. One who knew all your faults and loved you all the same.

He glanced over at Tanya, who was sitting beside him in one of the rows of chairs set up in the grounds of the Garrison harbourside mansion. She looked utterly gorgeous in her cerise chiffon dress, with its deep crossover neckline, floaty sleeves and long, softly layered skirt. There again, he'd think she looked gorgeous in anything.

Sensing his eyes on her, she turned her head and the most gloriously loving smile formed on her lips. 'See?' she said teasingly. 'That wasn't so bad, was it?'

He smiled. She knew him so well.

Fact was, she knew him better than anyone, even Richard. This past week they'd talked so much. He'd told Tanya the story of how he'd gone from being a waiter to the owner of Wild Ideas, without the benefit of higher education, using only his own imagination and ambition. He'd even found himself telling her about his past, and the beatings he'd received almost every night from his uncle. He'd endured the corporal punishment as part of his life, till the testosterone rage of adolescence—plus confidence in his own increasing size—had made him stand up for himself. He'd looked his uncle in the eye one night and told him if he touched him again he'd kill him. Something must have convinced the weasel that he meant it.

Even so, a month later, Harry had run away.

Tanya had listened to his story with a sympathetic ear and a big hug at the end of it.

'My poor darling,' she'd soothed, with cuddles and kisses. 'No wonder you've found it difficult to love and trust. But that's a long time gone and you've got me now. It's time to forget all about that. I love you. That's all you have to remember.'

He'd thought long and hard about what she'd said, but something still troubled him.

'Tanya…'

'Yes, darling?'

'Do you think I could be a good father?'

'I think you'd be a great father.'

'With *my* genes? My own father ran out on my mother and me, and my uncle was a bad bastard. Mean.'

'Harry, it's not written in stone that these things are passed on from father to son. You yourself said that as an adult you have to take responsibility for your own actions. If you *want* to be a good father, you will be. You're a fine man. And you don't have a mean bone in your body. You'd certainly be a good provider. And you have so much love in your heart left to give. Let's face it, you haven't used much of it up all these years, have you?'

'Is that a compliment or a criticism?'

'It's the truth.'

'And you still want to marry me?'

'In a minute.'

'I was thinking more of the New Year.'

'Oh. Oh, goodness.' He adored the flustered delight on her face.

'As much as I loved this simple garden ceremony, I have a hankering to get married in a church. The Femme Fatale factory will be closed for the Christmas break in January. Does Drybed Creek have a church?'

She blinked at him. 'You want to get married in Drybed Creek?'

'Of course. Tradition says you get married in the bride's home town. So! Does Drybed Creek have a church?'

'A small one. But there isn't a minister stationed there any more. One visits once a month.'

'That'll do. We'll work around that.'

'You do realise it will be very hot out there at that time of year.'

'Never fear. I'll have the church and pub air-conditioned.'

She gaped at him.

'Can't have my bride ruining her lovely white dress with perspiration stains, can I?'

'But it's such a waste of money!'

'The church can have portable air-conditioners, and I don't think the pub will be a waste. Arnie's decided to turn the place into a proper hotel after all, with rooms for tourists.'

'He never said anything to *me* about that.'

'I don't think he wanted to, because it was Dolly who convinced him it was a good idea.'

'Dolly!'

'You wanted him and Dolly together, didn't you?'

'Yes…'

'Then don't be a typical woman and change your mind.'

'I never change my mind.'

'Good. Now, do shut up and give me a kiss.'

'Here? With everyone watching?'

'No one's watching us. They've all toddled off to the marquee by the pool for pre-dinner drinks. We're the only ones still sitting here.'

'Oh. But you know what happens when you start kissing me. Things seem to get out of hand and we can't really… I mean…not here…'

'I'll find a way,' Harry said, and kissed her.

It was a challenge to find a private place with people milling all around the place. But Harry rose to the challenge. As usual.

He hoped whoever lived in the converted boathouse at the bottom of the garden wouldn't mind. But what a bed! And what a view! You could almost touch the water. It gave rise to an idea to buy his Tanya a house on the Harbour, with a jetty and a boat. Kids liked boats.

They were married in Drybed Creek's only church on the second of January. It was packed, and the temperature outside hovered about the forty mark, but inside it was a pleas-ant twenty-five. The raven-haired bride looked radiant in white and the groom couldn't take his eyes off her. The reception afterwards at the Drybed Creek Hotel lasted all day and all night, partly because no one wanted to leave the air-conditioning, but mostly because all drinks were on the house.

Arnie was prouder than any father-of-the-bride had ever been, and Dolly stood coyly by his side, planning to be a bride herself in the near future.

The bride and groom were only supposed to stay one night at the hotel before setting out the following day for Broken Hill airport and a secret honeymoon destination. But Tanya found it hard to say goodbye, as she always did, and this time Harry was similarly reluctant to leave. Being in love did make a place seem different. In the end he postponed their flash honeymoon for a week and stayed.

'You know, darling?' he said as he drew his wife into his arms that night. 'I've changed my mind. Drybed Creek *is* a romantic place, after all.'

'Mmm.' She smiled up at her new husband, thinking that any place Harry was would always be romantic to her.

'Is it all right by you if I don't use anything tonight?' he asked.

Tanya's heart kicked over. 'Are you sure, Harry? Really sure?'

'I've never been more sure of anything in my life,' he said. 'Just wanted to check with you first.'

'I want whatever you want, Harry.'

He smiled. And then he kissed her.

MILLS & BOON® PUBLISH EIGHT LARGE PRINT TITLES A MONTH. THESE ARE THE EIGHT TITLES FOR FEBRUARY 2001

---❧---

THE HUSBAND ASSIGNMENT
Helen Bianchin

THE BRIDE'S PROPOSITION
Day Leclaire

THE PLAYBOY'S VIRGIN
Miranda Lee

MISTRESS OF THE SHEIKH
Sandra Marton

RHYS'S REDEMPTION
Anne McAllister

GEORGIA'S GROOM
Barbara McMahon

SECRET SEDUCTION
Susan Napier

MARRIAGE IN MIND
Jessica Steele

MILLS & BOON®

Makes any time special™

MILLS & BOON® PUBLISH EIGHT LARGE PRINT TITLES A MONTH. THESE ARE THE EIGHT TITLES FOR MARCH 2001

———————— ❦ ————————

DELIVERED: ONE FAMILY
Caroline Anderson

THE HIRED FIANCÉE
Lindsay Armstrong

DON JOAQUIN'S PRIDE
Lynne Graham

THE PLEASURE KING'S BRIDE
Emma Darcy

SANCHIA'S SECRET
Robyn Donald

THE ENGLISH BRIDE
Margaret Way

THE DETERMINED HUSBAND
Lee Wilkinson

HIS VERY OWN BABY
Rebecca Winters

MILLS & BOON®

Makes any time special™